I0573005

# THEIR FOUR DATE
# EXPERIMENT

JEFF ADAMS

WILLIAM GAYHEART

*Their Four Date Experiment*
Copyright © 2025 by Jeff Adams & William Gayheart
All rights reserved.

*Their Four Date Experiment* is a work of fiction. Names, characters, places, brands, and incidents are solely the product of the author's imagination and/or are used fictitiously, though reference may be made to actual historical events or existing locations. Any resemblance to actual persons, living or dead, is entirely coincidental.

No part of this book may be reproduced in any form or by any electronic or mechanical means, including information storage and retrieval systems, without written permission from the author, except for the use of brief quotations in a book review.

# THEIR
## *Four Date*
# EXPERIMENT

JEFF ADAMS & WILLIAM GAYHEART

1

Theo

Zach Mendez strode onto the stage for his keynote at the ConnectSphere Expo. His presence was impossible to ignore—the crisp navy suit perfectly tailored, the precisely trimmed black hair, the designer glasses catching the light as he adjusted them with a practiced, almost too-smooth gesture.

A hush fell over the audience of tech devotees and industry insiders. He took his position center stage, a sleek confidence radiating from every movement.

A confidence that grated on me instantly.

"Love isn't a mystery anymore." His voice was warm and assured, designed to charm. "It's a science."

My pen pressed harder against my notepad, nearly tearing the page. Of course, that would be his opening line. Pure tech messiah arrogance.

The massive screen behind him illuminated with colorful graphs and statistics—LoveLogic's latest success metrics. Ninety-four percent satisfaction rate. Eighty-five percent of matches resulting in relationships lasting beyond six months. Seventy-eight percent reduction in time spent searching for compatible partners.

Numbers presented as gospel.

"We've mapped the emotional genome." Mendez continued pacing with measured steps, a predator patrolling his territory. His control was absolute. "Our algorithm doesn't just match people based on surface-level preferences. It predicts emotional compatibility through behavioral analysis and psychological mapping."

The audience nodded along, rapt. A woman two seats down sighed, a soft, worshipful sound that made my skin crawl. I resisted the urge to roll my eyes.

I'd spent six months digging into dating algorithms for my exposé. The investigation included tracking the digital wreckage of broken relationships, as well as interviewing people who were reduced to data points and left feeling hollowed out from the experience. Six months observing companies like LoveLogic commodify the most fundamentally human of experiences while calling it progress.

This guy, Mendez, was the most polished evangelist I'd encountered yet. There was an intensity about him, though, different from the usual Silicon Valley hype men.

He moved into the technical portion, explaining improvements to their patented "emotional compatibility mapping." His passion flared here—this wasn't just corporate speak. His hands, previously controlled, gestured more freely when discussing the algorithm's architecture, revealing the programmer beneath the CEO veneer.

The shift was subtle, but I noted it.

"We've increased predictive accuracy by seventeen percent this quarter alone." Genuine excitement broke through his composed facade. "The pattern recognition component now identifies compatibility markers that even users themselves aren't consciously aware of."

My phone vibrated. Vivian, my editor.

Vivian: *Is the tech messiah living up to the hype?*

I typed back quickly.

Theo: *Playing God with relationships and the crowd is eating it up. Q&A starting soon.*

Her response was immediate.

Vivian: *Remember, we need sound bites for the follow-up piece.*

I slipped the phone into my pocket. Mendez was concluding with user testimonials—slickly produced video clips of attractive thirty-somethings gushing about how LoveLogic had found their perfect match.

*The algorithm understood me better than I understood myself.*

*Love, optimized and sanitized.*

"We're not eliminating romance." Mendez's voice dropped to an intimate register that somehow made the cavernous hall seem small, personal. Everyone leaned forward. "We're optimizing the path to meaningful connection in a world where time is our scarcest resource."

A familiar tightness gripped my chest, sharp and sudden as memories surfaced. My father, clutching a printout from DateRight, his face alight with the certainty of "98% compatibility" with a woman twenty years younger. My mother, weeks later, her face pale against the pillow, the life seeming to drain out of her alongside her belief in thirty years of shared history.

This wasn't just professional critique for me.

The moderator opened the floor for questions. Several hands shot up.

Not mine. Not yet.

Mendez handled softball queries about timelines and partnerships, his answers polished, precise, occasionally even charming. He deflected challenges with practiced ease.

When the fifth consecutive question about investment potential came up, I raised my hand. The moderator scanned the room, perhaps seeking variety, and pointed my way.

I stood, ensuring my press badge was visible as I moved toward the aisle microphone. Recognition flashed across Mendez's face just before I spoke.

He knew who I was. Good.

"Theo Barrett, from *The Fulcrum*." My voice amplified through the hall, steady despite the adrenaline beginning to pulse in my ears. "In your presentation, you mentioned 'optimizing the path to meaningful connection,' but isn't there an inherent contradiction in reducing human emotions to data points?"

Mendez's posture straightened almost imperceptibly. The corner of his mouth twitched upward—not quite a smile, more like a boxer acknowledging an opponent stepping into the ring.

"Mr. Barrett. I've read your recent article." He adjusted his glasses, a gesture I was starting to recognize as a thinking pause, a control mechanism. "There's no contradiction when you understand that data doesn't reduce emotions. It illuminates patterns we're often blind to ourselves."

"In my research," I continued, gripping the microphone slightly tighter, "I interviewed dozens of people who felt dehumanized by algorithmic matching. One woman described feeling like 'produce being sorted on an assembly line.' How do you respond to concerns that systems like LoveLogic commodify what should be an organic human experience?"

A slight murmur passed through the audience. Mendez stepped closer to the edge of the stage, his focus all on me now, the polished CEO persona sharpening into something more intense.

"I'd respond that before algorithms, people were already commodifying each other—judging on appearance, social status, first impressions that often led nowhere." His voice remained measured, but a fire burned behind his words. The programmer defending his creation. "LoveLogic counteracts superficial sorting by highlighting compatibility factors people might otherwise overlook."

"But doesn't outsourcing our romantic choices to an algorithm diminish what makes human connection meaningful in the first place? The serendipity, the risk, the choice?"

"We're not outsourcing choice." A flash of

genuine frustration crossed his face before being controlled. "We're providing information. Better information than randomly bumping into someone at a coffee shop and mistaking physical attraction for compatibility."

I pressed harder, sensing the crack. "Your marketing materials claim 'LoveLogic understands you better than you understand yourself.' Isn't that explicitly encouraging people to trust an algorithm over their own instincts?"

The audience was fully engaged now, heads swiveling between us like spectators at a tennis match.

Mendez abandoned his position near the podium, moving to the edge of the stage, just ten feet from where I stood.

"Our algorithm processes thousands of behavioral data points that reveal patterns beyond conscious awareness." His professional polish fractured again, allowing the passionate developer to slip out. "Would you refuse an X-ray because it sees things you can't? Knowledge doesn't eliminate choice—it informs it."

"Knowledge isn't neutral when it's filtered through proprietary algorithms no one can examine. You're asking people to trust a black box with their emotional lives, based on data harvested through increasingly invasive means."

His eyes narrowed. "And you're romanticizing a status quo where people waste years in incompatible relationships because they trusted 'gut feelings' over objective compatibility assessment."

The moderator stepped forward, clearly sensing the escalating tension. "Perhaps we should move to the next question—"

Mendez held up his hand, a gesture of command that silenced the moderator.

"No, this is important." He looked directly at me, the audience forgotten. "Mr. Barrett, in your article, you characterized algorithmic matching as 'the death of authentic love.' But what's your alternative? Returning to a world where people make life-altering relationship decisions based on limited information and cognitive biases?"

"My alternative is that human connection isn't a problem technology needs to solve." My voice rang with conviction, fueled by more than professional skepticism. "The messiness, the uncertainty—that's not a bug in the system. It's a fundamental feature of authentic connection."

Mendez's expression shifted subtly—something unreadable flickered there, curiosity mixing with the frustration. "That's a lovely sentiment, but it doesn't explain why millions of people voluntarily use our service to find partners they might never have met otherwise."

"People also voluntarily use gambling apps designed to be addictive. Popularity doesn't equal ethics."

A ripple of uncomfortable laughter moved through the audience. Mendez's jaw tightened for a moment, then relaxed into an unexpected, almost challenging smile.

"Technology has always changed how humans connect, Mr. Barrett. From written language to telephones to dating apps. Each innovation was resisted by those who romanticized whatever came before." He spread his hands, reclaiming his stage presence. "I'm not claiming our algorithm is perfect, but we're using science to solve real problems of connection in an increasingly isolated society."

The moderator stepped in again, more firmly this time. "We do need to move on to other questions."

I nodded, relinquishing the microphone and returning to my seat, pulse pounding in my ears. On stage, Mendez smoothly transitioned to the next question. He regained his composure, but his eyes flicked toward me several times during his response.

He knew this wasn't over.

My phone buzzed.

Vivian: *Watching the livestream. That was GOLD. Call me when it's over.*

As the session concluded, I was aware of glances from nearby attendees. The conference schedule listed a networking reception next, where Mendez would no doubt be swarmed.

I hung back, observing from the periphery as he worked the room. Up close, away from the spotlight, smaller details emerged. The way he checked a vintage watch rather than his phone. How he listened with complete focus to whoever spoke to him. The intelligent intensity in his eyes as he discussed technical aspects with fellow developers.

There was something undeniably human about him in this setting, something his polished stage presence couldn't fully convey. Something that complicated the easy villain narrative I'd started building.

My phone rang. I stepped into a quiet hallway to answer.

"That confrontation is already trending," Vivian said without preamble. "The video clip hit fifty thousand views in twenty minutes."

"He's exactly what I expected." I glanced back toward the reception. "Brilliant, but detached from the human cost of what he's building."

The words felt less certain than they had an hour ago.

"The human cost is what we need to focus on for your book." Vivian's voice sharpened. "LoveLogic is the perfect case study—the most sophisticated algorithm with the most charismatic founder."

I watched as Mendez excused himself from a circle of admirers, stepping away to check something on his phone. For a brief moment, when no one was watching him, his confident posture relaxed. He pinched the bridge of his nose beneath his glasses, looking suddenly, profoundly tired.

"I want to dig deeper." My intensity surprised me. "Beyond the public confrontations. I need to understand what makes someone believe they can reduce love to an equation. What drives someone like him?"

"That's exactly what I wanted to hear," Vivian replied. "This could be the centerpiece of your manuscript. The philosophy behind the algorithm, direct from the source."

"I doubt Mendez will grant me an interview after today."

"Never underestimate the power of controversy. You clearly got under his skin." She paused. "And from what I could see, he got under yours, too."

I frowned. "What's that supposed to mean?"

"Just that there's nothing better for research than a passionate intellectual adversary." Vivian's smile was audible. "Get back to me with a plan for deeper coverage on LoveLogic. Your manuscript deadline isn't moving."

We ended the call, and I turned back toward the reception hall. Through the doorway, I caught sight of Mendez again. Someone had made him laugh—a genuine, unguarded expression that transformed his features.

Then, as if sensing my gaze, he looked my direction. Our eyes met across the distance.

Neither of us smiled or nodded. For three long seconds, we held each other's gaze, mutual recognition passing between us—intellectual adversaries sizing each other up across a battlefield of ideas.

I was the first to look away, turning toward the exit. This was just the beginning.

## 2

Zach

THE VIDEO of me sparring with Theo Barrett played on my tablet for the hundredth time. My face, tight with controlled frustration, stared back.

The clip had crested two million views overnight. Social media had already branded it #LogicVsLove.

My jaw clenched. I slid the tablet away, the sleek glass cool beneath my fingertips. "I've seen enough."

The conference room went silent. My marketing team exchanged glances across the polished table. No one seemed eager to break the silence.

Trina Alcott, my CMO and the closest thing I had to a friend who remembered me before LoveLogic, finally spoke. "The good news is you held your own. Statistically."

A weak attempt at humor. I didn't react.

"The bad news," she continued, "is this is the narrative Theo Barrett wants—faceless tech giant reducing love to cold data."

"I'm not faceless. I was standing right there. He was attacking the science."

And you. He was attacking you.

"That's not—" Trina exhaled slowly. "You know what I mean, Zach. This plays directly into his whole 'technology versus humanity' polemic."

I checked my watch—my father's vintage Omega, its familiar weight grounding me. Twenty-four hours since the confrontation. "What's the actual damage assessment?"

Trina tapped her tablet, projecting analytics onto the screen that hung on the wall. Crisp graphs replaced the city view screensaver.

"Social sentiment is split, but Barrett's audience is growing. Traffic to his original article quadrupled. Newsletter subscriptions jumped twenty percent." She swiped, another chart appearing. "Our new user sign-ups dipped eleven percent compared to what we'd expected after your talk."

A muscle ticked in my jaw. Eleven percent.

Quantifiable damage. "Temporary fluctuation. The algorithm's performance metrics—"

"The algorithm isn't the problem." Trina cut me off, a privilege reserved solely for her. "The narrative is that Barrett makes a compelling emotional argument. We need an equally resonant counterargument, grounded in human experience."

I took off my glasses, pulling the microfiber cloth from my pocket. The familiar ritual—clean, polish, replace—bought processing time. Conversations about narrative and emotion always felt like navigating poorly documented code. Messy. Prone to unpredictable outcomes.

"We present the data." I fit the glasses back in place. "Our success metrics. The improvements in relationship satisfaction."

A soft groan escaped from Ben Carter, the junior marketing associate at the far end of the table. He straightened when my gaze flickered his way, color rising in his cheeks.

"Sorry, Mr. Mendez," he mumbled. He shifted focus to the tablet in front of him. "It's just... Metrics don't connect. Stories do."

"Ben's right. You—"

Before Trina could finish, the heavy glass conference room door swung open. Daniel Park strode in, his bespoke suit radiating the kind of cold authority that made venture capitalists tremble and developers rewrite code overnight.

"I assume we're discussing damage control." He bypassed greetings entirely.

The air temperature seemed to drop. Daniel had led our Series C funding round. His firm held twenty percent of LoveLogic. He claimed the chair at the head of the table, and a ripple of discomfort passed through the team.

"We're addressing the Barrett situation." My voice was deliberately level.

"Good. Because the board is concerned." Daniel's manicured fingers tapped a precise, irritating rhythm on the table. "This publicity comes at the worst possible time. The IPO roadshow begins soon, and suddenly our founder is being painted as a soulless technocrat commodifying human emotion."

My stomach tightened. The IPO. Six years of effort. My life's work.

Negative press wasn't just noise. It was a direct threat to valuation.

"Barrett's criticism isn't new," I countered. "We've addressed these romantic objections before. The market understands our value proposition."

"The market invests in narratives consumers believe in." His voice was icy. "And right now, consumers are watching you struggle to defend whether your own product undermines real connection." He turned his sharp gaze on Trina. "What's the response strategy?"

She glanced at me, a flicker of solidarity before she answered. "We're developing several approaches. A data-driven campaign highlighting success metrics—"

"Worthless." Daniel cut her off. "Barrett's already framed metrics as dehumanizing."

"A testimonial series featuring successful couples—"

"Better, but defensive. Reactive." Daniel's gaze swung back to me, pinning me like a specimen under a microscope. "We need something bolder. Something that proves beyond doubt that our founder believes in his own product."

The room fell silent again. I knew instantly what he meant.

The logical conclusion, yet one I'd deliberately avoided for years.

"You want me to use LoveLogic personally?" I kept my voice devoid of inflection despite the internal alarms.

Daniel's smile was thin, sharp, with no warmth. "Nothing proves faith in a product like the founder using it. It's time, Zach. Your bachelor workaholic image was fine for the startup phase. Investors want stability. Commitment. A CEO who embodies the product's promise."

Seven years had passed since I learned how intimacy could be weaponized, how personal data could become leverage. The thought of putting myself back into that equation, exposing myself to that kind of vulnerability... my hand tightened on the chair's armrest. I forced it to relax.

Trina watched me, concern in her eyes. She knew. Not the details, but enough.

"I don't have time." The excuse felt flimsy even as I uttered it. The truth was the exposure, the risk of repeating... "We're three months from the biggest product launch in company history."

"Make time." Daniel's tone left no room for argument. "Or watch your valuation get cut in half by Barrett and his Luddite followers."

Silence descended again, thick and uncomfortable.

Daniel stood, smoothing his already perfect tie. "I have another meeting. I expect a concrete plan by end of day." He paused at the door, his parting shot delivered with surgical precision. "And Zach? Barrett's questioning whether anyone should trust an algorithm with their heart. Show them why they should trust the man behind it first."

The door swung shut with a soft clank, the sound disproportionately loud in the sudden quiet.

I exhaled slowly, a tension headache beginning. "Let's break for lunch. Reconvene at two."

The team filed out, relief evident in their postures. Only Trina remained, waiting until the room emptied before speaking.

"You knew this was coming eventually." Trina's voice was understanding, more friend than CMO. "You can't be the face of relationship technology and remain detached from it personally."

I moved to the window, needing the distance, the perspective.

The city below was a complex, interconnected system. Predictable, if you had enough data. Unlike human relationships. "I have relationships. Professional. Friendships. Family."

"You know what I mean." Trina joined me, her reflection appearing beside mine in the glass. "Look, I hate agreeing with Daniel Park about anything, but he's not wrong about the messaging problem."

"So I'm supposed to what?" The frustration I'd been suppressing broke through. "Let the algorithm pick someone and parade them around for investor confidence? A performance?"

Trina was quiet for a moment, thinking. Then her eyes lit up with the familiar spark that preceded either marketing genius or borderline insanity. "Actually, what if we turned this Barrett situation completely around?"

I turned from the window. "Explain."

"Barrett's criticism resonates because he's framed this as technology versus humanity, algorithm versus authentic connection." She began pacing, energized. "So let's change the narrative. What if we documented your process using LoveLogic? Show the human side of algorithmic matching."

"A publicity stunt."

"A transparency initiative," she corrected. "We show the real person behind LoveLogic using his own creation—doubts, process, the human element. It humanizes both you and the technology."

The vulnerability... Daniel would hate it. But the logic...

"Daniel wants proof I believe in the product. This gives him that while addressing Barrett's critique that we're hiding behind a black box."

She leaned against the window frame, facing me. "It's elegant, Zach. We take Barrett's biggest weapon and turn it into our strongest validation."

My internal cost-benefit analysis ran.

Personal cost: High.

Potential vulnerability: Significant.

Strategic benefit: Addresses Daniel's demand.

Counters Barrett's narrative. Demonstrates product faith.

Risk mitigation: Frame it as a controlled experiment. Define clear parameters. Minimize personal exposure.

It could work.

"Fine." The word felt heavier than it should. "Have Riley run my profile through the system and identify potential matches. We approach them discreetly. Limited dating arrangement, public documentation."

Relief washed over Trina's face. "I'll brief the team and get Riley started."

---

Two hours later, we reconvened. The tension from the morning had dissipated, replaced by the focused energy of a team executing a high-stakes plan. The marketing department presented a comprehensive campaign concept, "The Logic of Love: A Founder's Journey."

I listened, nodding at appropriate intervals while my mind constructed contingency plans.

A controlled experiment. Defined boundaries. Manageable risk.

I could use my own product, address Barrett's

criticisms with logic, satisfy Daniel—all without exposing myself to genuine emotional unpredictability.

"We need to move quickly." Trina pointed to social media trend charts. "The Barrett video is still driving conversation. We should announce within—"

A hesitant knock interrupted her. Riley Okafor, my lead algorithm developer, stood nervously in the doorway, tablet clutched to his chest like a shield.

"Sorry to interrupt," he said, shifting his weight. His usual slight dishevelment seemed amplified by anxiety. "You asked for the results ASAP, and, well..." He glanced around the room, eyes wide behind his glasses. "Maybe in private?"

Something in his expression made my stomach tighten. I nodded to Trina. "Let's take fifteen."

When everyone was gone, Riley approached the table.

"What's wrong?" I braced for system failure or data corruption. "Couldn't find any suitable matches?"

"No, we found matches." Riley's fingers tapped anxiously against the tablet case. "Multiple high-percentile matches. Your compatibility scores are robust, within expected parameters based on your profile metrics."

"Then what's the problem?"

Riley placed the tablet on the table, sliding it toward me as if handling radioactive material.

"This is your top match. 92% compatibility."

I looked down. The screen displayed a profile photo—intense eyes, prematurely salt-and-pepper hair, a challenging set to the jaw.

Theo Barrett stared back at me.

The floor seemed to tilt. "Impossible," I said, the word distant, unreal. "Run it again."

"I ran it three times." Riley's voice was barely a whisper. He pushed his glasses up. "Different parameter weights, cross-validation against alternate datasets. He comes up top every time."

I stared at the screen, the #LogicVsLove hashtag flashing in my mind with brutal irony. This couldn't be random. A cosmic joke coded into the universe.

"He's using a fake profile to manipulate the system." I grabbed at the most logical explanation. "Prove a point about algorithm vulnerability."

Riley shook his head, clearly miserable. "His profile predates your confrontation by over a year. Activity patterns, behavioral markers, psychometric indicators—all consistent with genuine use. And..." He hesitated. "The compatibility factors are legitimate, sir. Communication styles, value structures, intellectual approaches are all complementary in ways the algorithm prioritizes."

My programmer's mind took over, analyzing the breakdown displayed beneath the photo, seeking the flaw, the error in the code.

It wasn't a simple mirror match. The algorithm saw something deeper.

"This can't be right," I muttered, more to myself than to Riley.

"The algorithm doesn't make mistakes, Mr. Mendez." Riley echoed the phrase I'd used countless times myself. "It just sees patterns humans miss."

I'd made that exact argument to Barrett.

The door opened, and Trina returned. "The team's ready to finalize the announcement timeline —" She stopped, taking in Riley's pale face and my rigid posture. "Everything okay?"

Riley looked at me, eyes wide, silently asking for dismissal.

"Stay." I told him. Then, to Trina, "You need to see this."

Trina glanced between us, picked up the tablet, and scanned the screen. Her professional composure wavered for only a fraction of a second—a slight widening of the eyes—before snapping back into place.

"Well," she said after a long pause, setting the tablet down. "This is unexpected."

"It's a glitch." The word left a bitter taste in my mouth.

I wanted it to be a glitch. Needed it to be. But I'd said it myself more times than I could count that it doesn't.

"But the algorithm doesn't glitch," Riley and I said simultaneously. We exchanged a look—his apologetic, mine pure frustration.

Trina leaned against the table, processing. Then the inevitable strategist's smile spread across her face. "This is perfect."

I stared at her. "Perfect? It's a catastrophe. Barrett has been attacking our entire business model. He's publicly accused me of dehumanizing relationships."

"Exactly." Her smile widened. "And our algorithm—your algorithm—identified him as your most compatible match."

I saw the trajectory of her thinking. "Absolutely not."

"Think about it, Zach." Trina started pacing again, seemingly energized by the sheer audacity of the idea. "Barrett's whole critique is that algorithms can't capture human complexity. What better way to challenge his position than to demonstrate, publicly, that the algorithm sees something profound between its creator and its fiercest critic?"

"He'd never agree."

"He might." Trina wasn't letting it go. "He's writing a book. What better research than dating the founder of the company he's critiquing, using the very system he doubts? It's unprecedented access."

"This is insane." A reluctant fragment of my mind—the scientist, the programmer—was intrigued by the pattern the algorithm had detected.

Riley cleared his throat tentatively. "From a data-driven perspective, it presents a unique opportunity to validate the model under high-contrast conditions."

I shot him a look that could freeze helium. He shrank back.

"We propose a limited arrangement." Trina ignored the interruption. "Four dates. Documented for both his research and our transparency initiative. He gets unparalleled access. We get the ultimate demonstration of algorithmic insight."

"And if it's a disaster? If we demonstrate that we despise each other?"

"Then we've proven what we claim—that the algorithm identifies potential, but humans make the choices." Trina leaned forward, eyes bright with conviction. "Either way, Zach, we control the narrative again. And it creates the stories that Daniel Park and the board want to see. The social media exposure will be unparalleled."

I went through the motions of cleaning my glasses.

Professional advantages: Narrative control, investor reassurance, transparency demonstration.

Personal cost: Potentially astronomical.

"It's absurd," I said, the words feeling inadequate. "The man represents everything I've spent years fighting against."

"Passion is passion," Trina replied cryptically. "Maybe the algorithm sees beyond the surface antagonism."

"Or maybe this is how I destroy my company and my reputation simultaneously."

Trina's expression softened. "Zach, when was the last time you took a risk that wasn't meticulously calculated? What if the algorithm matched you with someone who challenges your entire worldview for a reason?"

I fell silent, the magnitude of her suggestion sinking in. Four dates with Theo Barrett. If Barrett and I could find even a fraction of the compatibility the algorithm predicted, despite our ideological chasm, it would be the most powerful proof of Love-Logic's validity imaginable.

"Fine." The single word costing more than any

venture capital negotiation. "Draft a proposal. Strictly professional. With limited engagement, clear boundaries, mutual benefit framing. And prepare for refusal."

Trina knew I couldn't resist the intellectual challenge. "I'll get legal working on the terms."

"And Trina?" I stopped her as she turned to leave. "Not a word about the ninety-two percent. Position this as a professional experiment to explore algorithmic compatibility under adversarial conditions."

Once I was alone, I stared at Barrett's profile on my screen. Complementary communication patterns. Shared core values beneath surface disagreements. Intellectual approaches that balanced each other.

For years, I'd trusted this algorithm with the romantic futures of millions. Defended it against critics like Barrett.

Now it had matched me with the human embodiment of that critique.

The scientist in me was captivated by the unexpected data point.

The businessman saw the strategic brilliance of turning adversary into case study.

But deeper down, the part of me that had built

LoveLogic not just as a company but as a shield—the part still scarred by Marco's betrayal—was terrified.

I closed Barrett's profile and straightened my tie, pushing the discomfort away with practiced discipline. This was a controlled experiment.

Nothing more.

I picked up my phone to call Daniel Park. He wanted proof I believed in my product? He was about to get it.

# 3

Theo

"Absolutely not." The words tore out of me.

I recoiled from the glossy folder Vivian Porter, my editor, pushed across her perpetually cluttered desk. LoveLogic's logo—that stylized heart twisted from ones and zeros—seemed to mock me.

I shoved my hands into my pockets, pacing the small space in front of the exposed brick walls of Vivian's downtown office. Gray skies pressed against the window, mirroring the storm brewing in my chest. "It's ridiculous. Did they even read the fifteen thousand words I wrote dismantling their entire business model?"

This proposal—this publicity stunt—felt like a

personal insult. Reducing human connection to data points wasn't theoretical for me.

"Please hear us out, Theo." Vivian leaned back in her chair, the picture of editorial authority in her sharp blazer, but a familiar gleam in her eyes betrayed her excitement. This wasn't just about the story for her. It was about the splash.

Across from her, Audrey Kim, my agent, crossed her legs, adjusting fashionably oversized glasses. Her impeccable suit jacket radiated effortless chic, a stark contrast to Vivian's creative chaos. "This isn't a date, exactly," she said. "It's a documented compatibility experiment."

"So fake dating." I stopped pacing to glare at the folder again. "Using their own flawed system? It's ridiculous."

"Your exposé is precisely why they want you." Vivian pushed the folder closer to me.

I ran a hand through my hair, frustration simmering.

Two days since I'd gone head-to-head with Mendez at ConnectSphere, the video clip bouncing around the internet like some intellectual cage match. My inbox was a war zone—interview requests, hate mail, speaking invitations.

And now this. A proposition designed to neutralize me, to make me a pawn in their PR game.

"Open the folder." Audrey's tone implied this was merely a business detail to be processed. "The terms are quite favorable."

Favorable? More like negotiating my ethical surrender.

Still, the journalist in me couldn't resist. I snatched the folder, flipping it open. Formal letterhead. Zach Mendez's precise signature likely digitized somewhere below.

Four public dates. Documented. Culminating in an exclusive piece for *The Fulcrum*.

"This is unethical on about six different levels," I mumbled as I scanned the legalese. "Compromising objectivity. Selling out my principles. Becoming a walking billboard for the very system I—"

"Gaining unprecedented access to the inner workings of the company you're critiquing," Vivian finished. She pushed away from her desk to the coffee station, asking if I'd like some.

"I've had four cups already," I replied, stomach churning.

Access. That was the insidious lure.

The chance to see behind the polished veneer, beyond the curated statistics. To truly understand—and expose—how LoveLogic worked. My fingers tightened on the folder. "It says here they want approval rights on anything I publish." A predictable corporate trap.

"Scroll down," Audry said. "We pushed back. They amended it to reviewing only for factual accuracy, not editorial content."

I turned the page. Redlined changes. Initialed concessions. My eyebrows shot up. "You've already negotiated terms? You knew I'd reject this."

Audrey offered an unapologetic shrug. "That's literally my job, Theo. Exploring possibilities."

"The publisher called this morning." Vivian returned with her steaming mug. "They're ecstatic and want to fast-track your book. Capitalize on the buzz. But they need more than outside criticism. They need first-hand experience. You, inside the machine."

Experience the machine? More like get swallowed by it.

I slammed the folder shut, crossing my arms. "It's a setup. LoveLogic wants to discredit me. Make me look like a hypocrite."

"Or they're calling your bluff." Vivian settled back into her chair. "You claim their algorithm is a black box? Now they're offering you a peek inside." Her logic was infuriatingly sound. "You can't accuse them of hiding their methods, then refuse when they offer transparency."

Damn her. I resumed pacing as the argument twisted inside me.

Professional opportunity versus personal principle. Unfettered access versus ethical compromise. And beneath it all, the nagging memory of my mother, the wreckage left by algorithmic certainty.

"It's a publicity stunt. A carefully controlled performance."

"Maybe," Audrey said. "But it's also a chance most journalists would kill for. Four dates with Mendez. Carte blanche to ask anything—on the record." She leaned forward, the scent of expensive perfume mixing with coffee aroma. "Think about the book. Instead of speculating, you get the founder explaining his philosophy directly to you. You get the human story behind the code."

I stared out the window, watching rain streak the glass. What kind of human story involved reducing connection to percentages?

"Why me?" I turned back to them. "They could have any tech journalist eating out of their hand. Why pick their biggest critic?"

Vivian and Audrey exchanged a look. Not a subtle glance, but a full-blown, neon-sign communication that screamed there's more.

Warning bells didn't just ring. They clanged.

"What aren't you telling me?"

Audrey cleared her throat, reaching for the folder again, flipping to a section I hadn't reviewed. "There's one additional detail. According to their proposal..." She paused, adjusting her glasses as if for dramatic effect. "LoveLogic ran Mendez's profile through their system as part of this transparency initiative. You appeared as a highly compatible match."

A harsh laugh barked out of me. "That's absurd."

"Ninety-two percent compatibility," Audrey said, unfazed. "Which is apparently in their top tier of potential matches."

The laughter died, choked in my throat. "Impossible."

"Apparently not." A smug look crossed Vivian's face. "Your profile has been active on their platform for research purposes, remember?"

I remembered setting up profiles on all the major platforms. Documenting the onboarding, testing functionality. I used accurate info for validity, but never, ever engaged. How could that data caricature of me match with him?

"Their algorithm is clearly flawed. This just proves my point."

"Or it proves theirs." Vivian leaned forward. "Either way, wouldn't you like to find out?"

I sank into the chair opposite her desk, rubbing

my temples. A cosmic joke. "LoveLogic's Biggest Hater: A Perfect Match?" The headlines wrote themselves, dripping with irony.

"The publisher is excited about this angle." Audrey pressed her advantage like a seasoned poker player. "They're talking about increasing the advance. Significantly."

My freelance writer's survival instincts twitched. Rent had just gone up. That money was already earmarked for bills, research, life. "How much?"

Another charged look between them.

"Thirty percent," Audrey said. "Plus expanded marketing support. A feature in *Wired*."

I whistled low. That kind of money bought time. Freedom. The ability to focus on the book without scrambling for side gigs.

"This is a mistake," I said. My conviction wavered, eroded by curiosity and financial pressure. "Mendez and I disagree on everything. We practically came to blows at the expo."

"Which is why this is fascinating." Vivian had yet another counter-argument. "Two opposing viewpoints. Forced engagement beyond sound bites. This is the heart of your book, Theo! Testing the algorithm in the most challenging scenario possible."

I picked up the folder again, staring at the glossy paper, the sterile font outlining this bizarre arrangement. Four dates. Public documentation. Equal editorial rights, supposedly. Playing right into their hands. Giving their system credibility.

Or—my journalist instinct offered helpfully—what better way to expose its flaws than from the inside? If the dates were disasters—and how could they not be?—I'd prove my thesis more effectively than any critique. Live, documented failure.

Another flicker of unwilling curiosity surfaced. Ninety-two percent? What twisted logic could possibly connect me to him?

"I maintain complete editorial control?" I asked again, needing the reassurance. "No matter how critical I am?"

"Full control," Audrey confirmed. "Review for factual accuracy only."

"And I can ask him anything? Algorithm, ethics, the works?"

"That's the deal," Vivian said. "Unprecedented access in exchange for participating in their experiment."

The professional opportunity was undeniable. The book's potential exploded with this angle. And the risk... if it failed, spectacularly, publicly? Maybe that failure was the best outcome for my argument.

"When do they need an answer?"

"Contract meeting scheduled for tomorrow afternoon," Audrey said smoothly. "Both legal teams, you, Mendez."

My stomach tightened. Facing him again so soon, not as adversaries across a stage, but as partners in this absurd experiment. That confrontation had left me strangely energized, his intensity a match for my own.

"I need to think about this."

"Don't think too long." Vivian's tone sharpened. "They offered it to you first. If you decline, they'll find someone else. Someone less likely to ask the hard questions."

That settled it. The thought of another journalist getting this story, someone potentially charmed or intimidated by Mendez, someone who wouldn't push back—it was intolerable.

"Fine. I'll do it. One additional condition."

"Which is?" Audrey poised her stylus above her tablet.

"I want the compatibility analysis. The real data breakdown, not just the percentage. If I'm taking part in this charade, I need to know what their damn algorithm thinks it sees between us."

Vivian smiled, a predator sensing victory. "Consider it added to the agreement."

LoveLogic headquarters gleamed, a monument of glass and steel reflecting the afternoon sky back at itself.

Inside, the reception area assaulted the senses with sleek surfaces and a wall-sized display pulsing with real-time "success metrics." Match rates, message exchanges, relationship longevity stats presented like digital trophies.

It disgusted me.

I tugged at the collar of my shirt. Dark jeans, vintage band tee, navy blazer—my attempt at bridging journalistic skepticism with corporate formality. The touchscreen check-in flashed a message: *Welcome, Theo Barrett. Trina Alcott will escort you momentarily.*

Right on cue, frosted glass doors slid open. A woman with a razor-sharp geometric bob and impeccable red lipstick approached. Trina Alcott, chief marketing officer. I recognized her from industry photos—Mendez's right hand, the architect of LoveLogic's carefully curated image.

"Mr. Barrett." Her handshake was firm. "Thank you for considering our proposal."

"Still considering," I corrected, my voice sharp. "That's what today's meeting is for."

I followed her through the glass doors, feeling like I was stepping into enemy territory.

"Of course." Her professional smile didn't waver. "We're excited about the potential collaboration, regardless of your past critiques."

"Those critiques stand."

We entered an elevator sleek enough to belong on a starship. Images of sickeningly happy couples flashed across the walls—LoveLogic propaganda. I focused on keeping my expression neutral.

"I'd be disappointed if they didn't." Trina pressed the button for the thirtieth floor. "This arrangement only works if both perspectives remain authentic."

Right. As authentic as a reality TV show.

I'd spent last night digging deeper into Mendez—his background, patents, that unusual psychology co-major alongside computer science. The man was more complex than the tech bro caricature, which somehow made this whole situation feel even more dangerous.

"Zach's already in the conference room." Trina gestured for me to exit as the doors swooshed open onto a floor of polished concrete and glass walls. "Along with our legal team and your representatives."

Through the glass, I saw them. Audrey and our lawyer. Across the long table, two suits guarding LoveLogic folders. And at the head, Zach Mendez, focused on a tablet, looking less like a stage performer and more like a CEO.

He glanced up as we approached. Our eyes met through the glass. A jolt, unexpected and unwelcome, shot through me.

Neither of us looked away.

Trina opened the door. "Everyone's here. Shall we begin?"

The next hour was a blur of legalese. Clause by clause, contingency by contingency. Publicity rights, content approval, scheduling parameters.

They dissected our potential interactions like a corporate merger. The clinical language stripped away any pretense of human connection.

Mendez and I exchanged few words, mostly clarifying technical points for lawyers. But the air between us crackled with unspoken tension—adversaries contractually obligated to simulate compatibility for mutual gain.

"Now, regarding the compatibility data," Audrey said, reaching my added condition. "Mr. Barrett requires access to the full analysis."

A subtle tensing in Mendez's shoulders. Had I hit a nerve?

"That information is proprietary—"

Mendez cut off one of his lawyers with a raised hand.

"We can provide a detailed report." His gaze met mine across the table. No projection, just quiet certainty. "A breakdown of the major compatibility factors, omitting the proprietary weighting algorithms. Similar to premium user access, but more comprehensive."

"That's acceptable." I matched his neutral tone. "As long as it provides meaningful insight beyond generic statements."

A ghost of a smile touched his lips. "I assure you, Mr. Barrett, our algorithm doesn't deal in generics."

"Then we're in agreement," Trina said. "Shall we discuss the proposed date schedule?"

Four dates. Two weeks.

Technology museum. Cooking class. Literary event of my choosing. Restaurant finale.

"Neutral territory," Trina explained, "for a balanced experience."

"Neutral territory for the battle of ideologies?" The question slipped out, sharper than intended.

Mendez looked up from his tablet, his dark eyes pinning me. "Not a battle, Mr. Barrett. An experiment."

"An experiment presupposes objectivity. Which I doubt either of us possesses here."

"Then perhaps 'exploration' is the appropriate term." Was that amusement in his eyes? Or annoyance? "Unless you're approaching this with predetermined conclusions?"

"I have six months of research." I gripped my pen tighter. "And a lifetime of believing human connection requires more than data points."

"Yet you're here." The simple words landed with surprising force. "Curiosity overcoming conviction?"

Before I could formulate a response that didn't betray my internal turmoil, Audrey intervened. "I believe we've covered all substantive terms. If both parties are satisfied..."

Documents slid across the polished table.

I scanned the final version, Audrey's checks already noted.

Signature line. My name waiting to be written.

I hesitated. Committing to spend time, documented time, with the man whose life's work represented everything I critiqued. The man whose algorithm claimed that we were compatible.

Across the table, Mendez watched me, his own pen poised.

"Second thoughts, Mr. Barrett?" His voice was quiet, almost intimate in the sterile room.

I met his gaze, steeling myself. "Just considering the irony of signing a contract for something most people approach organically."

"Most contracts attempt to manage unpredictable human behavior," he said, the philosophical framing unexpected. "Dating is perhaps the most unpredictable behavior of all."

A smile almost broke through my resolve. Instead, I pressed the pen to the paper, signing my name with a deliberate, perhaps overly firm, flourish.

"There." I slid the document back across the table, the action feeling both anticlimactic and monumental. "Let the experiment begin."

Mendez signed his copy, his signature as precise and controlled as everything else about him. When he looked up again, something new crossed his expression—not triumph in completing the agreement. Was it vulnerability?

"The compatibility report will be delivered this evening," he said, all business again. "First date on Friday. Abbott Technology Museum. Ms. Alcott will coordinate."

The meeting dissolved into handshakes and professional pleasantries. As people gathered brief-cases and files, I found myself face-to-face with Mendez near the door.

"Why this? Why me? Your biggest critic?"

He pulled a cleaning cloth from his pocket and wiped his glasses before speaking. "Perhaps the algo-rithm sees something we don't."

Before I could decipher that cryptic remark, his

legal team whisked him away. I watched him go—perfect posture, efficient movements, impenetrable composure.

Riding the elevator down, alone, the weight of my decision hit me. Four dates with Zach Mendez. A contract binding me to the heart of the system I wanted to expose. Four chances to challenge him. Four opportunities to prove human connection defied computation.

My phone buzzed.

Vivian: *Contract signed?*

I typed back, staring at my reflection in the elevator's mirrored wall.

Theo: *Signed. First date on Friday. Either proving my thesis or becoming the world's biggest hypocrite.*

Her reply was instantaneous.

Vivian: *Or both. That's what makes it interesting.*

4

Zach

IF ANYONE ever needed proof of how far I'd go to keep my company viable and profitable, this was it.

The stylist Trina had insisted on—I needed to be "more approachable," she'd chirped—had swapped my perfectly tailored navy suit for a charcoal blazer over a cashmere sweater I wouldn't have chosen. The material was soft and unstructured. My hair, normally precise, had been mussed into something "less controlled." Even my glasses felt wrong— marginally different frames that supposedly made me look "more intellectual, less corporate."

I adjusted them again, the unfamiliar weight awkward on the bridge of my nose. Less corporate, maybe. More like an actor playing a part.

"You look great." Trina leaned against the polished chrome doorframe, tablet poised.

I smoothed the sweater, the fabric too soft beneath my fingertips. "I look like I'm playing a role in a commercial."

"That's essentially what this is." Trina ticked something off on her screen, ignoring my unease. "An infomercial for LoveLogic's human side."

The door swung open, and one of Trina's marketing associates entered carrying a garment bag like a sacred relic. "The backup outfit, Mr. Mendez. In case the museum is colder than expected."

A backup outfit? For a two-hour museum visit?

I pinched the bridge of my nose—harder than necessary. "Are contingency garments truly required?"

"We need to be prepared for all possibilities," Trina replied, already turning away. "Now, the talking points. Again."

Trina's team had repurposed the conference room, transforming it into a PR command center. The digital board displayed photos of the Abbott Technology Museum, suggested conversation prompts, and a schedule broken down into excruciating 15-minute increments. It all made my head hurt.

I sank into a chair, the expensive cashmere suddenly feeling constrictive.

Trina distributed printed notes.

"Three key messages." She highlighted them on the screen with a laser pointer. "One, the human element behind LoveLogic's technology. Two, the scientific validity of emotional compatibility mapping. Three, the transparency of our methodologies."

"This is ridiculous." I muttered, scanning the suggested responses to Barrett's potential challenges. "I'll sound like a corporate automaton."

"You'll sound like a CEO defending his company's value, which is exactly what you are."

The door opened again. Riley entered, his nervous energy a stark contrast to everyone else's calculated calm. "Sorry I'm late." He pushed his glasses up. "I was finalizing the compatibility breakdown you requested for Mr. Barrett."

Trina waved him in. "Perfect timing. Zach was just reviewing the talking points for the date."

Riley hovered awkwardly. "Actually, I was hoping to speak with Zach privately about some of the metrics before the, um, compatibility experiment." His eyes darted towards me.

Trina glanced at her watch. "Fifteen minutes. Wheels up at 12:30 sharp."

She ushered the others out, leaving Riley shifting his weight.

"What is it?" I braced for a problem with the report. "An error in the metrics?"

"No, not at all." Riley took the seat opposite me. "That's what I wanted to show you. The compatibility factors between you and Mr. Barrett are... statistically distinct."

I leaned back, weariness settling over me. "You don't need to sell me on the validity of this. I've already agreed to the experiment."

He slid his tablet toward me, his nervousness replaced by the focused intensity he usually reserved for code.

I glanced at the screen—a complex matrix of compatibility factors, clusters color-coded.

"Your surface preferences are almost diametrically opposed," he said. "Activities, social patterns, daily routines. Minimal overlap. But your core compatibility derives from complementary traits, not shared ones."

"Meaning?"

"You challenge each other in constructive ways." As he discussed the data, his excitement increased. "Your communication styles differ, yet match in intensity and depth. Your value systems, while appearing contradictory, prioritize the same underlying principles, just through different frameworks."

"This could be confirmation bias."

"We tested for that. You and Mr. Barrett balance each other. Your structured approach complements his intuitive way of working, and vice versa."

"What he lacks is an understanding of how technology enhances human connection," I said dryly.

"Actually, the data suggests his perspective on human connection might enhance your understanding of technology." He caught my skeptical expression and backpedaled. "Not that your understanding isn't already exceptional. Just differing viewpoints creating cognitive synergy. That's what the algorithm detected."

Before I could process that, Trina returned, trailed by the stylist.

"Car's waiting," she announced.

As we descended in the elevator, a strange tightness formed in my chest. Not anxiety—I'd pitched billionaires, testified before Congress.

This was different. Why did the prospect of two hours with Theo Barrett make the sweater feel too warm, my perfectly mussed hair feel artificial?

"Zach, I know this is far from your comfort zone," Trina said as we arrived at the lobby. She spoke just loud enough that only I'd hear her. "This is good for the future of your company. Remember, this isn't about winning an argument. It's about showing the human face of LoveLogic."

More like performance art. A stage-managed attempt to counter Barrett's critique of dehumanization by enacting an over-scripted version of human interaction.

The irony was uncomfortable. I nodded, my jaw tense.

---

THE ABBOTT TECHNOLOGY MUSEUM sprawled along the renovated waterfront, a monument of glass and steel reflecting the cold afternoon sun. Our driver bypassed the public entrance, pulling up to a discreet side door where a museum representative waited with an almost unnervingly cheerful smile.

"Mr. Mendez, welcome," she greeted us. "We're honored to host this special visit. The relevant exhibits are ready, and we've ensured the space allows for comfortable conversation and optimal visual capture."

Translation: roped-off areas and managed sightlines.

"Mr. Barrett arrived five minutes ago." She led us

through polished side corridors. "He's waiting in the Emerging Technologies hall."

I saw him before he spotted me.

Barrett studied a neural network visualization, absorbed.

His posture was relaxed, leaning against the railing in a way that suggested he'd find a way to be comfortable in any environment. Dark jeans, a vintage band t-shirt I didn't recognize beneath a well-worn leather jacket—casual but intentional. His hair looked genuinely tousled, not styled.

He turned as we approached, and our eyes met. That intensity again—a focused presence that seemed to cut through the artifice of the situation. A slight, unwelcome jolt went through me, which I quickly pushed away.

He offered his hand. His grip was firm, warm. "Mr. Mendez. Right on schedule."

"Thank you again for accommodating this experiment."

An awkward beat stretched between us, filled only by the low hum of the exhibits. We were acutely aware of the arranged nature of this encounter. The museum guide rushed to bridge the silence with over-eager explanations of what we'd see on the tour, while Trina exchanged polite murmurs with Barrett's editor nearby.

"Shall we begin with the AI Ethics installation?" The guide gestured toward an interactive display mapping algorithmic decision-making. "It connects wonderfully to LoveLogic's user-centered design philosophy."

Barrett raised a questioning eyebrow, but followed without comment. As we walked, I registered the discreet click of the photographer's camera from a calculated distance.

The performance had begun.

The exhibit examined how algorithms make decisions—and how human biases shape them. "This highlights potential programming bias," the guide explained. "Even subtle weights in initial parameters can impact final outcomes."

Barrett turned to me, his gaze direct. "An interesting starting point. Does LoveLogic worry about bias in its matching algorithms?"

Here it was—the first question. My talking points dictated a pivot to rigorous testing protocols, diverse development teams. The script was inadequate for what I needed to say.

"Every algorithm reflects the biases of its creators. The critical question isn't whether bias exists, but how actively we identify and mitigate it." I imagined Trina's disappointment that I'd already abandoned her plan.

Barrett looked taken aback for a fraction of a second. "And how exactly do you do that with something as subjective as compatibility?"

"By continuously testing against real-world relationship outcomes, not just theoretical models. The algorithm refines itself based on longitudinal success metrics."

"Ah, but your definition of 'success'?" Barrett continued the line of questioning, clearly engaged beyond polite necessity. "Longevity? Satisfaction scores? Absence of conflict? The metrics themselves embed value judgments about what relationships should be."

He had a point—one I'd wrestled with during LoveLogic's early development. The scripted response involved holistic success measurement. The honest approach seemed more necessary. This wasn't a typical interview.

"That's a legitimate challenge. Our initial metrics were too simplistic, prioritizing longevity. We've since evolved more nuanced indicators of relationship health."

He studied me, assessing my candor. Was this genuine or sophisticated public relations? "Such as?"

"You can see growth patterns in how communication changes. We observe conflict resolution methods by analyzing how they interact. We measure adaptability based on how they respond to outside life events." I moved toward the next display, which visualized decision pathways. "Human relationships aren't static. Compatibility changes. Our latest algorithms recognize that."

Barrett followed, his expression thoughtful. "But the core assumption remains—that relationships can be optimized through data analysis."

"Not optimized." I held his gaze to make my point. "Enhanced. The algorithm doesn't create connection—it identifies significant potential."

Our conversation deepened as we moved through the hall, diverging further from Trina's schedule. Barrett's questions were sharp, probing the underpinning of LoveLogic's methodology, but they lacked the overt hostility I'd expected. I found myself explaining technical nuances that I rarely discussed publicly.

The museum guide and our handlers trailed behind, exchanging uneasy whispers as our dialogue intensified. Our energy exceeded the bounds of a controlled publicity event.

Our intellectual sparring continued through holographic innovations, quantum computing displays, and the human-machine interface galleries. At some point, Trina had abandoned attempts to redirect us, now watching with a mix of professional worry and personal fascination.

The schedule dissolved into two full hours consumed by debate.

I countered his romanticization of serendipity with data on relationship inefficiency. "The average person spends years cycling through incompatible relationships. That's not romantic—it's inefficient and often painful."

"But those 'wasted' years are formative. The struggle builds resilience. Your algorithm might match effectively, but it risks removing the very challenges that strengthen connection."

"It removes unnecessary friction," I clarified. "It doesn't guarantee perfection—it increases the probability of meaningful connection."

He studied me, his gaze direct, piercing the professional distance I tried to maintain. "Have you used it yourself? Before this publicity arrangement?"

Talking points suggested pivoting to LoveLogic's mission. A shadow—Marco's face, betrayal sharp and sudden—flickered in my mind before I suppressed it.

"No. I haven't."

"Why not?" The challenge in his eyes wasn't accusatory, just curious.

I thought of ways around it. Again, the truth seemed simpler, but I couldn't give the entire story.

"Limited time, primarily. Building the company required my full focus."

"Convenient." His single word response hit closer than I liked. "Creating a system for others while keeping yourself safe and removed from the emotional equation."

Before I could say anything else, Trina stepped between us. "I'm afraid we're over our scheduled time. The museum will close to the public soon."

Barrett checked his watch, genuine surprise flashing across his face. "Two and a half hours already?"

The realization startled me as well. The engagement had been consuming. Time had passed unnoticed.

As we walked toward the exit, Barrett fell into step beside me, the earlier tension gone.

"For what it's worth," he said, "that was more substantive than I expected."

"Disappointed you didn't get to expose the soulless tech mogul?"

He smiled slightly—a genuine, unguarded expression that softened his features. "The day's not over. I still have plenty of material for my critique."

"I have no doubt." A smile almost slipped out, but I managed to suppress it.

Outside, our cars waited, engines idling. The

photographer captured a few final, staged images as we exchanged professional goodbyes. Barrett's editor looked satisfied. Trina maintained her composure, though I detected calculation in her eyes.

"Until the cooking class," Barrett said as we parted.

"I'll try not to burn anything," I replied, an attempt at lightness.

His expression shifted, registering the unexpected change in tone. "I make no such promises."

As my car drove away, Trina was already scrolling through social media analytics on her tablet. "Well." Her voice was carefully neutral. "That was... not the plan."

I pulled at the neckline of my sweater. "Was it a disaster?"

"Not exactly." She angled the screen toward me, displaying trending topics. #TeamLogic versus #TeamLove. Clips of our debate spreading rapidly. Passionate user arguments echoing our own. "Engagement is significantly higher than projected."

I scrolled through the comments, registering the intense investment from both sides. They weren't reacting to a publicity stunt. They were engaging with the core philosophical conflict.

"So, not a failure."

"Not in terms of visibility." Trina's tone shifted

to concern. "But Zach, you went off-script, which could be a liability. The talking points—"

"Were artificial," I finished. "He would have seen through them immediately."

She studied me for a long moment, her gaze missing nothing. "You enjoyed it, didn't you? The debate."

I started to issue a standard denial, then paused. The intellectual engagement had been compelling.

"It was stimulating. Barrett asks challenging questions."

"And the 92% compatibility makes a little more sense," she said, a knowing glint in her eyes.

I leaned back against the leather seat, weariness hitting me. "Don't start. Intellectual engagement doesn't equate to personal compatibility."

She wisely dropped the subject, turning back to her data analysis. But as the city blurred past the windows, I replayed moments from the museum— the sharpness of Barrett's intellect, the unexpected humor, the genuine curiosity beneath his critique.

For a carefully constructed performance, it had felt surprisingly real.

# 5

Theo

MY KEYS CLATTERED on the coffee table's surface, the sound loud in the quiet of my apartment.

The nearly three-hour debate with Zach Mendez had left a strange buzz humming in my brain, a disorienting mix of adrenaline and something I couldn't name and didn't want to examine too closely.

Collapsing onto the sofa, I scrubbed both hands through my hair, trying to physically dislodge the memory of his intense focus, and the unexpected flashes of passion when he defended his creation.

I'd gone in ready for a fight, prepared to expose the cold logic behind LoveLogic's promises. And I had fought. But it hadn't felt like a simple victory. It hadn't felt simple at all.

My gaze landed on my laptop, open on the desk, the blank document glaring back at me.

I needed to write and try to translate the intellectual showdown into the narrative I'd been building for months: tech mogul treats human connection like debugging code. Cold, analytical, detached. The perfect villain for my articles and the book.

Except...

I pushed off the sofa, pacing the small space between the overflowing bookshelves and the stacks of vinyl records. My apartment, usually a comforting chaos, seemed constricting.

I sat at the desk, fingers hovering over the keyboard.

*Zach Mendez coldly deflected questions about emotional nuance, retreating into technical jargon...*

Delete.

Coldly? No, that wasn't right.

He'd engaged, fiercely at times. His passion for the algorithm's architecture had been undeniable and genuine at the same time.

*The LoveLogic CEO, detached from the human cost, presented optimization as connection...*

Delete.

His frustration when I pushed him about algorithmic certainty hadn't come across as detached. It had seemed personal. Annoyed, yes, but engaged. Maybe even a flicker of vulnerability before his shields snapped back up?

Dammit. I slammed my fist lightly on the desk.

Why was this so hard?

He was the embodiment of everything I argued against. Why couldn't I articulate that?

What I'd witnessed—the controlled intensity, the flashes of the developer beneath the CEO, the surprising willingness to debate ethics beyond talking points—it refused to fit neatly into the box I'd built for him.

My phone rang, the sharp sound cutting through my thoughts.

Mom.

Perfect. If anyone could reset my perspective and reinforce the necessary skepticism, it was Diana Barrett.

"Hey, Mom." I dropped back onto the sofa's worn cushions.

"There you are." Her voice carried the familiar warm, slightly distracted tone of someone mid-thought. "I saw the clips from that museum stunt with the algorithm man. How did it really go?"

The phrase "algorithm man" grated somewhat, but I pushed that away. "His name is Zach Mendez."

"I'm aware." The edge was subtle but present in her voice, a reminder of the raw nerve this subject touched. "Zach Mendez. Brilliant, I'm sure. Convinced he can map the human heart with code."

"It's a bit more complex than mapping." I immediately regretted my choice of words.

"So you're taking his side now?" Surprise sharpened her tone.

"No, I just—" I sighed, standing again to pace. "It's complicated. The visit wasn't what I expected."

"Meaning?" Papers rustled. She was no doubt grading tests or papers.

"He wasn't easy to dismiss. I expected a corporate drone spouting marketing lines. Instead, I got substance. His grasp of behavioral psychology, the way he defended the core concepts—it was more thoughtful than I anticipated."

"Theodore James Barrett." The use of my full name stopped me cold. "Need I remind you what happened when your father trusted an algorithm over thirty years of lived experience?"

Guilt washed over me at the pain still simmering in her voice, two years later.

"I haven't forgotten," I said quietly.

"He dismantled our lives because a system told him to." The paper rustling intensified. "And now you're spending time with the man who represents the epitome of that same dangerous promise. You looked intensely engaged as you talked to him."

What had been posted? I went to my laptop and searched for my name.

Sure enough, the tech blogs had already dissected the visit.

One image showed Mendez and me near the neural network display, leaning toward each other, captured mid-debate. The caption read: *Tech Visionary Zach Mendez and Critic Theo Barrett: A Meeting of Minds.*

Another showed us examining a holographic interface, standing closer than I remembered. The focus on Zach's face was striking—open, intense, nothing like the controlled expression he usually wore. Seeing it captured... it was disturbingly accurate to the intensity that'd been in the room.

"It's all performative." I closed the browser window, trying to convince myself as much as her. "A PR stunt. I'm gathering research for the book."

"Just be careful, Theo." Her voice softened, the familiar maternal worry replacing the academic sharpness. "These tech visionaries are incredibly persuasive. They sell certainty in an uncertain world. That's a powerful lure."

Her words clarified the unease that had been growing since I'd left the museum. LoveLogic wasn't just selling matchmaking. It was selling the alluring, dangerous illusion of certainty in the messy, unpredictable realm of human connection.

"You're right." My resolve solidified, the purpose of my book sharpening again. "And that's the danger I need to expose."

"Good." Relief flooded her voice. "Because for a moment there, you sounded confused."

We talked for another twenty minutes about university politics and her latest research, the familiar territory helping to focus me. But after hanging up, the confusion lingered.

Before I could get back to work, my phone buzzed with a text.

Vivian: *Need your first impressions for tomorrow's online piece. Keep it sharp.*

I stared at the message, then at the blank document. The sharp, easy critique felt dishonest.

Finally, I began to type.

*The encounter with LoveLogic founder Zach Mendez presented a challenge. Expecting a detached technocrat, I found instead a passionate defender of his creation, articulate in both its technological intricacies and its intended human benefits. While fundamental disagreements about the ethics of algorithmic intervention in relationships remain, the museum visit revealed a complexity—in both the man and the machine—that demands deeper examination.*

It wasn't the fiery takedown Vivian wanted, or the neat narrative I'd planned. It was something messier, more true.

I continued writing, detailing our arguments, Zach's unexpected candor, the unsettling flashes of warmth beneath his controlled exterior. As I typed, my attention drifted to the compatibility report Mendez had provided. I'd barely glanced at it, dismissing it as irrelevant PR.

Pushed by an unwilling curiosity, I opened the file.

*Communication Patterns: Complementary Styles (Analytical/Intuitive). High potential for generative discourse.*

*Intellectual Approach: Shared Value for Rigor, Differing Methodologies (Systematic/Contextual). Potential for mutual growth through challenge.*

*Core Values Alignment: High congruence on principles of Integrity and Authenticity, despite differing expressions.*

I scrolled through the analysis, comparing the algorithm's detached pronouncements with the reality of our debate.

Generative discourse? At the time, it'd seemed more like intellectual combat.

Mutual growth through challenge? Maybe.

Unsettlingly, some of the algorithm's points resonated with moments from our time spent together.

I closed the file abruptly. Flawed data from a flawed system. Yet...

The cooking class was next. Neutral territory, according to their proposal. Another stage for our performance. But a different thought surfaced, unwelcome but persistent. There was an opportunity to not just critique, but to understand. To push past the CEO persona and see if the complex, contradictory man I'd glimpsed at the museum was the reality.

The prospect was both professionally necessary and personally terrifying.

6

Zach

THE MUTED GLOW of the quarterly projections reflected off my glasses, but the numbers wouldn't coalesce.

Instead, all I could think about was Theo Barrett's face—the intensity in his eyes during our museum debate, the unexpected directness of his challenges. He hadn't dismissed my arguments. He'd engaged with them, dissected them with a frustratingly accurate insight.

It was stimulating but also unsettling. A familiar resistance coiled in my gut at the thought of the next phase of this performative experiment. The cooking class. Another carefully orchestrated facsimile of compatibility.

A scent announced him before the knock—Daniel Park's aggressive sandalwood cologne, a precursor to the inevitable wave of pressure. I minimized the projections and straightened my tie, bracing myself as he entered without preamble.

"The board still has concerns." He settled into the chair opposite me, radiating calculated authority.

"Good morning to you too, Daniel."

He placed his phone on my desk, screen up, displaying a still image from the museum. Barrett and I, leaning toward each other, captured mid-argument. The headline above it read: "LoveLogic's Mendez and Critic Barrett: More Friction Than Chemistry?"

"This was supposed to demonstrate your algorithm's effectiveness." Each word was precise as a surgical incision. "Instead, social media is buzzing about your intellectual sparring match. #LogicVsLove hasn't died down. We can't afford a pre-IPO stumble like Venturi Tech had last year."

I removed my glasses, reaching for the cloth in my desk drawer. A few seconds were required so I could process and control my rising irritation.

This wasn't just about the IPO. It felt like being forced back into an equation I'd distanced myself from years ago.

"User engagement has actually increased nearly

fifteen percent since yesterday." I replaced my glasses. "The debate format is generating more interest than a standard publicity tour would have."

"We're not looking for 'interesting,' Zach. There's less than two months before the IPO." Daniel's manicured fingers drummed a precise, disturbing rhythm against my desk. "We need 'reassuring.' 'Stable.' 'Proven.'"

"The algorithm is proven. Six years of data, millions of successful matches—"

"I'm not talking about the algorithm." Daniel's interruption was harsh. "I'm talking about you. The board agreed to this publicity stunt because it was supposed to show you engaging with the product. Demonstrating its effectiveness through your own experience."

I studied him, the polished veneer barely concealing his irritation. "That's exactly what I'm doing." The words came out strained.

"No, you're debating philosophical differences about technology while investors wonder why Love-Logic's founder can't manage a simple date with his supposed 92% match." Daniel leaned forward. "The next outing needs to show actual compatibility, not intellectual conflict."

My watch showed 8:47. Too early for the headache forming behind my eyes, a tight, pulsing ache already starting. "What do you want from me, Daniel?"

"I want you to take this seriously." His voice lowered, intensifying the pressure. "The cooking class tomorrow is an opportunity to show how your algorithm identifies complementary styles."

"You want me to pretend there's a personal connection?" The words tasted like surrender.

"I want you to stop sabotaging the possibility of one." He stood, straightening his already immaculate suit. "The pre-IPO pricing analysis is underway. Every public perception data point matters."

After he left, the cologne replaced by sterile office air, I went to the window to stare at the city skyline. Six years—from dorm room concept to multi-billion-dollar valuation—and now everything hinged on my personal performance in a glorified reality show. The absurdity didn't escape me, but neither did the crushing weight of expectation.

"THESE PARAMETERS NEED TIGHTENING." I pointed to a section of code on Riley's screen later that night. "The confidence interval is too wide."

Riley nodded, making the adjustment. It was after nine, the algorithm development lab hummed with the focused energy of a late-night coding session —a welcome escape from the performance demands pressing down on me.

"Better?" Riley asked.

I studied the revised code. "Yes. Run a simulation with the Berlin dataset to verify."

While Riley initiated the test, I leaned back, rubbing my eyes beneath my glasses. This work grounded me. It was controllable. Unlike the prospect of tomorrow.

"How are you feeling about the second date?" His voice was casual.

"It's not a date," I corrected automatically. "It's a documented compatibility experiment for publicity purposes."

"Right. Of course. The, um, compatibility experiment." He paused. "I've been analyzing the interaction data from the museum."

"Riley..." I braced for more pressure.

"Your communication pattern with Mr. Barrett precisely matches what the algorithm predicted." Enthusiasm overrode his usual deference, something that happened more often in the past few days. "Complementary cognitive frameworks, productive tension, generative dialogue."

Productive tension. Is that what kids were calling it nowadays?

"We argued for hours." I pushed the unwelcome flicker of scientific curiosity away.

"Exactly!" Riley's excitement rose further. "The algorithm doesn't prioritize agreement—it identifies engagement potential. Your conversation exhibited all the markers of high intellectual compatibility."

I turned back to the monitors, needing the anchor of the algorithm's code. "That's meaningless in this context. Barrett opposes everything LoveLogic represents."

"Actually, opposition to a concept doesn't necessarily indicate incompatibility with the person behind it."

The lab door opened, and Trina entered, still in work clothes, coffee in hand.

"Still optimizing?" She settled into a chair beside me.

"Final adjustments," I confirmed. "Preparing for tomorrow?"

"Precisely." She slid her tablet in front of me. "A more structured approach for the cooking class."

I skimmed the bullet points—conversation prompts, staged interactions, suggested moments for "natural laughter." The artificiality grated. "No. I'm not following a script this time."

"The museum was compelling but confrontational." Trina was unfazed by my rejection. "The class needs to show compatibility." She paused, studying me for a moment. "Look, Zach... this seems to be getting to you more than the usual PR demands."

"It's a distraction," I muttered.

"Or maybe you're reacting to having your professional creation challenged so directly, so personally." She stopped. But when I said nothing, she continued. "You actually listened to him. Understanding his background could help you counter his arguments more effectively. Or, understand why this is affecting you differently."

Learning more about Barrett's motivations might offer a strategic advantage, a way to anticipate his lines of attack.

Professional preparation. Nothing more. "Fine. It can't hurt to gather more data on his viewpoint."

After Trina and Riley left, I remained. Trina's suggestion echoed in my brain. I hadn't approached Barrett as a variable to be understood, but an obstacle to be managed. A strategic error.

I opened my laptop and started a systematic search—Theo Barrett, beyond the industry critiques.

His author archive at *The Fulcrum* revealed broader interests—features on community resilience after tech disruption, profiles of people rebuilding human connection in digital environments, essays on the value of inefficiency in creative processes. His writing was insightful, often poetic, and deeply humanistic without being technophobic.

I dug deeper, finding older articles from his early career. A piece about his Connecticut childhood in a household of academics. Mentions of psychology professors as parents. I also discovered an unexpectedly personal essay about his father leaving his mother for a younger woman—a relationship initiated through DateRight, one of our competitors.

The story contained no direct references to algorithmic dating platforms, but the subtext was clear. Barrett's skepticism wasn't merely philosophical—it was born from witnessing personal devastation.

I sat back, processing this new information. The passionate opposition I'd encountered at the museum now appeared in a different light. Not just intellectual disagreement, but something much more personal.

I turned my attention to Barrett's compatibility report, studying it with fresh eyes. According to our metrics, both of us showed unusually high scores in "principled conviction"—the willingness to defend deeply held beliefs. We also shared "elevated empathy markers" despite expressing that emotion through different frameworks—his through narrative connection, mine through systematic problem-solving.

Our surface differences were substantial, but the algorithm had detected complementary patterns beneath that contrast, just like Riley said.

Barrett's critique came from witnessing pain caused by algorithmic certainty misused. My creation of LoveLogic had been driven by wanting to prevent pain from mismatched connections.

Different approaches to a shared concern.

I closed the report, uncomfortable with the direction of my thoughts. This was a publicity arrangement, nothing more. Barrett's personal history explained his professional position, but didn't alter our fundamental disagreement.

For the cooking class, I would approach Barrett with a better understanding of his perspective. Not to win an argument or perform for cameras, but to engage genuinely with the human behind the criticism.

# 7

Theo

THE AIR HELD a damp chill as I hurried toward the upscale cooking school. Copper pots gleamed with an almost aggressive warmth in the window, mocking the gray weather, reflecting the sleek, professional-grade appliances visible through the glass.

A small gaggle of photographers had already gathered outside, huddled under umbrellas. It was confirmation, if I needed it, that our "compatibility experiment" remained a spectacle.

Zach stood near the entrance, checking his watch —that vintage Omega I'd noted before, a distinct analog item in his digital world. He looked different. Less like the *algorithm man* I kept trying to pigeonhole.

He'd dressed down in dark rinse jeans that probably cost more than my rent and a charcoal Henley beneath a structured, casual blazer. Even from this distance, I sensed his contained energy, the precise, scanning way he observed the street.

Our eyes met as I approached him, and his posture straightened, a shift from observation mode to engagement.

"Right on time." He extended his hand. The gesture was oddly formal after hours of intense debate at the museum, a step back into prescribed roles.

"I'm predictably unpredictable." I shook his hand. His grip was firm, warm despite the chill air.

A hint of a smile touched his lips. "An oxymoron."

"Or a paradox. Depends on your perspective." I nodded toward the gleaming doors of the cooking school. "Shall we?"

Inside, stainless steel workstations gleamed under bright, clinical lights. It smelled cleaner, sharper than a typical kitchen—more lab than hearth.

A chef with an impressive waxed hipster mustache and eyes that betrayed immediate recognition greeted us, his professional smile tight. The PR teams had orchestrated everything. We'd have private instruction in a glass-enclosed section, visible to the photographers outside like specimens in a terrarium, but insulated from their intrusion.

"Today we're preparing carne asada with chimichurri and roasted vegetables." The chef led us to a workstation that resembled a surgical suite more than a kitchen. "Each of you will prepare your own version, following the same basic recipe."

Our stations were meticulously organized—ingredients pre-measured in sparkling glass bowls, utensils arranged by size, recipe cards laminated and propped against the stainless-steel backsplash as if they were commandments. I watched Zach survey the setup, his eyes cataloging the arrangement with a flicker of approval.

"Perfect," he murmured. He washed his hands with methodical, ritualistic precision at the adjacent sink.

I followed suit, the contrast between us already sharp. Where he moved with deliberate efficiency, each action predetermined, I instinctively looked beyond the arranged ingredients, wondering what possibilities might be hiding in the kitchen pantry.

The chef demonstrated the basic techniques—knife skills, searing temperatures—then left us to work. He retreated to observe, along with representatives from our teams, from just outside our glass enclosure.

Zach reached for the recipe card, studying it with intense concentration before touching a single ingredient.

"Not going to wing it?" I was already grabbing the garlic, the papery skin crackling under my fingers. I ignored the small bowl of pre-minced cloves and started chopping an entire head, the pungent aroma rising instantly.

Zach glanced at my cutting board, a subtle crease appearing between his brows. "The recipe calls for two cloves. You've cut at least four."

"I like garlic." I went back to work, the rhythmic thump-thump-thump of the knife a familiar comfort. "Recipes are suggestions, not an instruction manual. Like roadmaps, maybe, but you choose the detours."

"They're formulas refined through testing," he countered. He precisely measured a teaspoon of olive oil. "Consistent inputs yield consistent results."

"And consistent results yield consistent bore-dom.". I drizzled a generous pour of oil into my bowl, eyeballing the amount. The scent, grassy and rich, bloomed in the air. "Food should surprise you. Have personality."

Zach paused, setting down his measuring spoon. He watched me work, his expression unreadable for a moment. Was that fascination or disapproval behind the glasses?

"You approach cooking the same way you approach relationships, I suspect. Intuition over structure."

"And you approach both like debugging code." I nodded toward his orderly arrangement, the perfectly diced onions in their neat pile. Damn him, even his knife skills were precise. It would be easier if he fit the detached tech-bro box I'd built for him.

Rather than taking offense, he considered this, tilting his head. "Structure creates reliability. Reliability builds trust."

"Spontaneity creates discovery." If he wanted to speak in simplistic, feel-good meme clichés, I was okay with that. "Discovery builds connection."

I tossed herbs into my bowl without measuring, crumbling the leaves between my fingers, releasing their fragrance.

A photographer appeared at the window, camera raised, lens aimed at us. We noticed him simultaneously, the spell of our banter breaking. The performative aspect of our arrangement snapped back into focus, sharp and unwelcome.

For several minutes, we worked side by side, absorbed in our tasks. I watched Zach from the corner of my eye, struck again by how elegantly he moved through the recipe, each motion deliberate, fluid, economical. He handled the heavy chef's knife with unexpected grace, his perfect cuts a stark contrast to my more rustic chop. There was a focus in his movements, a tactile engagement that was different from his usual analytical distance.

"You've done this before," I said.

"Cooking?" He didn't look up from slicing peppers into perfect strips. "Yes."

"I figured you for someone with a meal delivery service," I teased. I tried to reclaim our earlier rhythm. "All pre-portioned ingredients and minimal effort. Maximum efficiency."

"That would be efficient." A small, almost involuntary smile played at his lips before vanishing. "But cooking is one of the few activities where I don't mind inefficiency."

The admission surprised me more than it should have. "Really? Why's that?"

He hesitated, his knife pausing mid-slice. He seemed to weigh his words, deciding on the appropriate data to share.

"It's... meditative. Tactile. Grounding. Present in a way that most of my work isn't."

I hadn't expected that answer. Was that genuine, or a calculated move to seem more human? The sincerity resonated, catching me off guard, chipping another piece from the simplistic narrative I'd tried to maintain. What kind of stress required this sort of tactile escape?

"What about you?" he asked. He turned the question back to me as he moved his prepped ingredients toward the stove.

"My mother." I followed with my haphazardly chopped vegetables. "She believes recipes stifle creativity. That measurements are tyranny." The memory brought a warmth—uncomplicated and real. "She taught me to cook by smell and taste. Trial and error."

"That explains your approach." He arranged his strips of meat in the hot pan with geometric precision. The controlled sizzle rose, a clean, contained sound.

I tossed mine in more haphazardly, the pan spitting and hissing in protest. The rich aroma of searing beef filled the space. "And who taught you? Culinary school? Private lessons from a Michelin-starred chef?"

"My grandmother." His voice softened, the word almost catching. "Mi abuela."

My mental dossier on Zach Mendez, compiled from corporate profiles and tech articles, contained algorithms and funding rounds, not abuelas.

As he flipped the meat with precision, I recognized a specific method—a quick, controlled flick of the wrist that distributed the searing heat perfectly across the surface.

"That's a comal technique." The observation escaped before my internal editor could intervene.

Zach looked up, genuine surprise clear in his expression. "You recognize that?"

"I traveled through Oaxaca for a story a few years back." A small, unexpected satisfaction crept in. Surprising him felt good. "Spent time with families in rural kitchens, learned traditional cooking methods. That wrist flip is distinctive. Ensures an even crust."

Something shifted—a subtle opening, like a tightly locked door cracking just enough to let in a wash of light. The CEO facade dissolved, replaced by a warmth that felt almost personal.

"My abuela would be impressed you noticed." This time the smile reached his eyes, erasing the careful control for a beat. "She insisted there was a right way—her way—to flip meat. Said you could taste the difference."

"Could you?"

"Absolutely." His smile continued, genuine and unguarded. "Though I never admitted it until I was much older. Children aren't supposed to concede that their grandparents are right about anything."

I laughed. "Universal truth across all cultures."

Our conversation flowed more naturally after that, moving between cooking techniques, the merits of cilantro, and unexpected childhood memories prompted by smells and tastes. The performative politeness that had marked the start of our meeting began to dissolve, replaced by something that edged dangerously close to genuine engagement. Even the ever-present photographers outside faded from my awareness.

As we plated our finished dishes, the contrast was striking.

My plate featured generous, slightly messy portions arranged with casual artistry—a riot of color and texture. His displayed precise plating with architectural balance, vegetables fanned out like spokes on a wheel.

"Two approaches, same ingredients," I said.

"Different executions of the same concept." He studied both plates with analytical interest. "Which do you think tastes better?"

"Only one way to find out." I grabbed two clean forks from the utensil holder. "Taste test. Scientific inquiry."

Zach hesitated only briefly, a flicker of his usual caution, before accepting a fork. We each tried the other's dish, and I watched his expression as he sampled mine, trying to decipher the micro-expressions beneath his controlled approach to flavor.

"Too much garlic?" I asked. I was unable to resist a smile.

He chewed thoughtfully before answering. "Perfect amount of garlic." Surprise colored his tone. "But inconsistent salt distribution."

"Yours is technically flawless," I acknowledged after tasting his creation. He'd cooked the meat and balanced the flavors perfectly. "But a little safe. Like a peer-reviewed study."

"Safe?" His eyebrow raised in familiar challenge. "I think you mean reliably executed."

"I mean you could have been bolder with the spices. Taken a risk."

Instead of defending his precise methodology, Zach surprised me again by considering my critique, glancing back at his plate. "Perhaps. The algorithm always identifies areas for potential optimization."

"Not everything needs an algorithm, Mendez." The familiar argument surfaced, but without the earlier edge.

"On that, we continue to disagree, Barrett."

The challenge was still there, but with an added note of playfulness.

The chef returned to evaluate our dishes, diplomatically praising both while highlighting different strengths—my flavor intensity, Zach's technical execution.

---

As we cleaned our workstation side by side, the movements comfortable, almost synchronized, a sharp crack of thunder sounded overhead. We turned toward the windows. Rain, which had only threatened before, was suddenly pouring down, sheets of water obscuring the view, drumming against the glass with sudden fury.

"Perfect timing," I said dryly. I glanced at my phone to check the weather app. A solid wall of red and yellow stretched across the radar map. "Looks like it's settled in for a while."

Zach frowned, checking his watch—that intrinsic need for quantifiable data asserting itself. "My driver isn't scheduled to return for another thirty minutes."

"I was planning to walk," I said. "My apartment's about fifteen blocks from here."

"In this?" He gestured toward the downpour.

Another crack of thunder, closer this time, answered his question. The cooking school staff began bustling around, closing windows, pulling down awnings, the storm disrupting the planned order of the afternoon. The photographers and even members from the publicity teams were gone. Somehow I'd missed that. It was surprising they'd actually left us alone.

"I can call for a car earlier." Zach reached for his phone without hesitation, defaulting to logistical solutions.

"In this weather, you'll be waiting at least half an hour, anyway." I glanced toward the drenched street. "There's a decent coffee shop around the corner. We could wait it out there. Unless you need to get back to optimizing relationship futures?"

Uncertainty flickered across his face—this deviation wasn't part of the scheduled program. I hoped he'd agree, curious to continue our conversation away from the performance aspects of our arrangement.

"Alright." He gathered his jacket. "Coffee sounds like a reasonable contingency plan."

We made a dash through the rain. The thirty seconds it took left us drenched and somewhat breathless as we ducked into the small cafe. Half-empty and glowing with warm yellow light, the space offered a stark contrast to the storm outside. The air was rich with the aroma of coffee and baked goods. We settled at a corner table far from the windows, shedding our damp jackets.

"Not quite the planned conclusion to our culinary compatibility assessment." Zach ran a hand through his wet hair. The precise styling was gone, replaced by a more natural, slightly tousled look that made him appear younger, less armored.

"I thought spontaneity created discovery," I replied with a smile. I echoed my earlier words as I wiped rain from my face with a napkin.

After ordering coffee, we sat in a quiet peace for a moment, the drumming rain creating a soundtrack that insulated us from the world outside. The performative pressure faded.

"So your abuela taught you to cook." I broke the silence once our drinks arrived. The warmth seeped into my chilled fingers. "Tell me about her."

The question seemed to catch him off guard again.

I saw him mentally cycle through potential responses. He wrapped both hands around his mug, his gaze softening.

"She was... formidable." The word was chosen with his usual precision but delivered with unusual warmth. "Immigrated from Mexico with almost nothing. Worked cleaning houses for decades. Raised five children essentially alone after my grandfather died young. She believed in precision, discipline, excellence in everything. No excuses."

"Sounds familiar," I said without thinking. The parallel to his own approach was striking.

He glanced up, acknowledging the similarity. "I suppose it does. But she was equally fierce about family, connection, legacy. Her recipes were strict measurements on paper, but they were stories in practice. Each dish had history, context."

There was genuine affection in his voice. A glimpse of the deep human attachments that shaped the algorithm creator. It sparked something in me—a recognition that this was more than a story of critic versus creator.

"What about your mother?" His focus shifted back to me. "You said she taught you to cook by instinct?"

"She's a psychology professor. She believes strict rules inhibit authentic expression. Cooking was her rebellion against the constraints of academia, her way of embracing creative chaos."

"Interesting." He studied me. "So your approach to food is shaped by intuitive rebellion, while mine comes from honoring structure as a form of legacy."

"I hadn't thought of it that way," I admitted, stunned by the insight. "But yes. That feels accurate."

The conversation shifted deeper as the rain continued, creating a cocoon of shared space and unexpected honesty. I shared stories about my mother's kitchen experiments—some spectacular failures as well as accidental masterpieces born from pantry scavenging. Zach listened with focused interest, asking thoughtful questions, his usual professional distance replaced by curiosity.

"After my parents separated, cooking became even more important to her. A way to reclaim joy, control, something tangible when everything else felt like it was falling apart." My throat tightened as I spoke—words I hadn't planned to share, drawn out by the intimacy of the moment.

Why was I telling him this? The man who built these systems needed to hear the human cost... or was I just making excuses because he was actually listening?

"That must have been difficult." His voice was quieter, softer than before. Not pitying, only acknowledging.

"It was." I traced the rim of my coffee mug, the ceramic still had some warmth beneath my fingertip. The memory coiled my chest—Mom's pale face against the pillow, the bewildered hurt in her eyes. "Especially how it happened."

Zach waited rather than pushing for more. His stillness created a space that made me continue, needing to share the context for my critique.

"My father met someone through a dating app. DateRight, not LoveLogic," I clarified quickly. "He walked away from a thirty-year marriage because the app told him they were ninety-eight percent compatible."

Understanding dawned in his eyes, sharp and immediate. His usual analytical lens seemed momentarily offline, replaced by... empathy? "And that's why you critique algorithmic matching so passionately."

"Part of it." My chest tightened with the admission. "I watched my mother—brilliant, loving, complicated—reduced to a failed data point in someone else's equation. It felt like violence by spreadsheet."

Zach was quiet for a long moment, his gaze distant. "I'm sorry that happened. That's not what these systems are meant to do."

"But it's what they can do." My words lacked the sharp edge that would have been just a few days ago. "They offer the illusion of certainty in an uncertain world. That's seductive, especially to people looking for easy answers."

"They offer information," he corrected gently. "Not certainty. Data to inform choice, not dictate it. The mistake is treating probability as guarantee."

I studied his face, struck by the conviction in his expression. "Is that distinction clear to users? Or does the marketing promise more?"

"Not always." His admission was small but significant. "Perhaps not obvious enough."

A flash of unexpected validation surfaced, tempered by skepticism. He saw the flaw—at least part of it.

Before I could respond, Zach redirected—maybe to safer ground.

"My abuela used to make caldo de res—beef soup—whenever I was struggling with something." A nostalgic warmth entered his voice. "She claimed it could solve any problem, from coding bugs to existential dread. When I was coding the first version of LoveLogic in my dorm room, pulling all-nighters, fueled by caffeine and imposter syndrome, she'd send huge containers of it through my cousin who lived nearby."

"Did it help?" I pictured a younger, less polished Zach sustained by soup and ambition.

A genuine, almost boyish smile spread across his face. "I built a billion-dollar algorithm, didn't I?"

I laughed, the sound blending with the rain against the windows, the tension easing between us again. "Correlation doesn't equal causation, Mendez."

"Says who?" He leaned forward, eyes bright with unexpected playfulness. "Maybe my abuela's soup contains pattern-recognition enhancers science hasn't identified yet."

"Now who's being intuitive rather than data-driven?"

As the downpour began to ease, our conversation drifted between personal stories and philosophical questions with a rhythm that was unexpectedly natural—unforced, unscripted. Before I realized it, thirty minutes had passed.

"It's finally letting up." Zach glanced toward the windows, where the streetlights gleamed off slick pavement.

"So it is." A peculiar disappointment settled in my chest, a reluctance to end this unscheduled conversation.

He checked his watch. "My driver should be here by now."

We gathered our still-damp jackets and moved toward the door. Outside, a sleek black car waited at the curb.

"I can drop you home." Zach's offer hung in the moist air.

The proper response—the objective one—would be to decline, maintain professional distance. "Thanks. That would be nice."

The car's interior was luxurious, all quiet leather and polished chrome, the privacy partition already raised. As we settled into the plush seats, I became acutely aware of how small the space felt, charged with the residue of our unexpected conversation.

"Your address?" Zach asked. His phone was poised, returning momentarily to logistical efficiency.

I gave him my cross streets, and he relayed the information to his driver through a text.

"This wasn't what I expected," I said after a moment of silence.

"The rain?"

"The conversation." I turned to face him in the dim interior light. "When I agreed to this arrangement, I thought it would be entirely performative. Adversarial, even."

Zach studied me with a thoughtful expression. "And now?"

The truth felt risky and necessary. "I'm not sure what it is."

Something shifted in his eyes. "It's still an arrangement, Barrett." His voice regained some of its professional distance. "There are clear parameters and a defined purpose."

"Of course." I looked away, stung by the reminder. "The scientific approach."

As the car moved through rain-slicked streets, neither of us spoke. The silence wasn't uncomfortable, but layered with unspoken questions, possibilities simmering just beneath the surface. When we reached my street, Zach's driver pulled to the curb.

"Thank you for the ride." My hand hovered over the door handle.

"Thank you for the cooking critique," he replied. And that small, almost smile appeared again. "Perhaps I'll be bolder with spices next time."

The simple statement—next time—suggested future interactions beyond the prescribed dates. I nodded in acknowledgement.

"Good night, Theo."

"Good night, Zach."

We'd used first names.

That subtle shift stuck with me as the black car pulled away, disappearing into the glistening night.

# 8

Zach

I STARED out my office windows as my mind drifted back to the cooking class, Theo's easy laughter, the unexpected intimacy of the rain-soaked conversation afterward.

Compatibility, the algorithm had predicted. It hadn't predicted this startling lack of focus.

My phone vibrated, and I reached for it.

Theo: *Quick question—in your ConnectSphere presentation, you mentioned "pattern adaptability" in relationship evolution. Direct quote for citation purposes?*

Just business. Research. I typed a response, forcing professional detachment.

Zach: *Advanced algorithms don't merely extrapolate from past behavior—they identify pattern adaptability, predicting not just static preferences but how people respond to new situations.*

I set the phone down, turning back to my computer. Before I could open the document I needed to work on, another text came through.

Theo: *Thanks. Though "merely" feels unnecessarily defensive. Your algorithms do extrapolate from past behavior—that's their foundation.*

A smile tugged at my lips. Even through text messages, he challenged me.

Zach: *The adverb emphasizes that our approach goes beyond simple extrapolation. It's precision, not defensiveness.*

Theo: *If you say so. Linguist friends would call that a hedge word.*

Impossible. My fingers were already moving.

Zach: *Do all your friends analyze language patterns, or only the ones you consult when messaging me?*

Theo: *Only the ones I need to impress with my rigorous texting methodology.*

The notification dots appeared, vanished, reappeared.

Theo: *Is that what you're doing? Trying to impress me?*

A direct query requiring careful calibration.

Zach: *I'm still processing that data point as well.*

Theo: *Always the scientist. Enjoy your processing. I have an editor breathing down my neck. See you at 2.*

I put the phone face down on the desk. The echo of his words—*always the scientist*—lingered longer than it should have.

"You seem different today," Trina observed from the doorway.

"Different how?" My hand went to my glasses, an involuntary adjustment.

"Less contained." She frowned slightly. "You were humming earlier. Definitely humming."

"I don't hum."

"My point exactly." She came in and took a seat across from me. "Does this have anything to do with Theo Barrett coming in today for an office tour for research purposes?"

When the request had come in yesterday, an immediate protective instinct flared—LoveLogic headquarters was my domain, meticulously designed, completely controlled. The thought of Theo observing it, analyzing it, finding flaws... it created an unwelcome tension. The risks of revealing too much.

But refusing would contradict the transparency narrative and violate our agreement.

My only response was to raise an eyebrow.

Trina took the hint to move on. "I arranged the media tour route."

The standard route showcased polished surfaces and metrics, hiding the messy, complex reality of the work. Suitable for investors, perhaps, but not for someone like Theo. He'd see through the performance.

Trina laid out the folder detailing the route and talking points. "Key messages are highlighted, and selected team members have their briefing notes."

I flipped through the schedule. "Thirty minutes in the innovation lab, but only ten in the algorithm development center?"

"The innovation lab photographs better. And the dev center contains sensitive information."

I looked up from the polished plan, a restless energy rising within me. "The development center is the heart of what we do. Hiding it feels dishonest."

Trina's tone shifted. "Are you sure this is wise, Zach? Your interactions with Barrett go off-script. Giving him access to the core algorithm workspace meant significant risk—proprietary information, potential for negative portrayal."

Not to mention the exposure—on a personal level.

Marco flickered at the edge of my thoughts—the effortless charm, the feigned interest that had hidden betrayal. I pushed it back. Theo wasn't Marco. The risk was different—not of exploitation, but of being seen for who I really was.

"I'm aware of the risks," I said, words clipped. "But Barrett isn't just any journalist. He'll recognize if we're trying to hide something. Transparency requires showing the process behind the polished output." I closed the folder. "I'll handle the development center portion myself. No script."

"Zach, you're trusting him with more than most people ever get. Just make sure he knows what that means."

Her words lingered as I instructed the development team—necessary precautions, but no deliberate attempt to hide the nature of the work itself. By two o'clock, I'd orchestrated an environment that allowed for authenticity within secure parameters.

When reception buzzed—*Theo Barrett has arrived*—I checked my reflection, straightening my already straight tie. A flicker of irritation at my own uncharacteristic behavior surfaced.

Get a grip, Mendez.

He stood in the lobby, more professional than I'd

seen him before—dark jeans, a crisp button-down under his leather jacket, bag slung across his shoulder. His eyes met mine, perceptive as always.

"Welcome to LoveLogic." I extended my hand, noting the slight tension in my posture.

His handshake was firm, warm. "Appreciate the access."

"Research access was part of the agreement." I gestured toward the security gates, defaulting to professionalism. "Shall we begin?"

The initial stages of the tour proceeded according to the familiar script. I outlined our company structure, mission, and user growth metrics. Theo asked sharp, insightful questions, making occasional notes in a small, worn notebook. He observed everything, not just the curated displays but the interactions between employees, the subtle environmental cues.

"Your workspace design is interesting," he remarked as we walked the executive floor. "More human-centered than I expected. Less sterile pods, more collaborative spaces."

"What were you expecting? Engineers plugged into the matrix?"

He smiled, a genuine expression that crinkled the corners of his eyes. "Something closer to that, yes. This has warmth."

"We design algorithms to strengthen connection between people." For once, the standard line didn't sound rehearsed. "It would be counterproductive to work in an environment that inhibits it among our own team."

We reached the innovation lab, a space designed more for impressing visitors than facilitating actual work. Holographic displays pulsed with abstract data flows, animations depicted connections forming across gleaming global maps.

"This is where we visualize large-scale interaction patterns." I recited the approved description while bracing for Theo's inevitable critique of its superficiality.

He walked into the room, taking it all in. "It's beautiful." He stopped before a dramatic holographic swirl. "Stunning. But also quite theatrical, wouldn't you say?"

"What do you mean?"

He gestured around the space. "These displays are designed to convey complexity without revealing specifics. It's impressive stagecraft. The real work happens somewhere less photogenic, I assume?"

His perception cut straight through the corporate veneer. "You're not wrong." Relief accompanied the admission. "This is the showcase. What we show investors who want to *see the algorithm* without understanding the underlying code."

His eyebrows rose, acknowledging my candor. "So, where does the actual work happen?"

The question hung there—an invitation. Even though I'd planned to take him to the dev center if he'd asked, I couldn't deny that it meant revealing something authentic, and a level of access that few people outside of LoveLogic had.

I met his gaze, seeing not just journalistic curiosity but genuine intellectual interest. "Would you like to see?"

Surprise flickered across his face, quickly followed by that intense focus I recognized and had grown to appreciate. "Yes. Very much."

We bypassed the planned route, taking the elevator to the restricted twenty-eighth floor. As the doors opened onto the algorithm development center, I swiped my security badge, the decisive click echoing.

The energy was different here—less polished sheen, more focused. Programmers worked at multi-screen stations, and dense, complex equations covered the whiteboards.

"This is where the actual algorithm development happens—construction, not stagecraft." Pride coursed through me as I showed him around. "No holograms, just code, coffee, and the occasional existential debate about free will versus algorithmic determinism."

Theo took it all in, his eyes bright, missing nothing. "It feels more real here. Alive."

"It is." I nodded to a few team members, registering their curious glances. "Everything downstairs is the packaging. This is the engine."

As we moved into the space, Alicia waved me over from her workstation. "Mr. Mendez? Quick question about the Brussels dataset anomaly?"

I hesitated, aware of Theo observing this impromptu interaction—deviating from any semblance of a planned tour.

I went to her station. "Show me."

Alicia, barely a year out of her PhD program but already one of our sharpest analysts, turned to her monitor. "This clustering behavior—it only emerges when we adjust the emotional vulnerability threshold within a very narrow range. It's impacting the adaptive communication weighting."

I leaned in, absorbed by the complexity of the pattern, the elegance of the unexpected correlation. "Excellent catch, Alicia."

"Standard procedure doesn't cover this specific variable interaction," she said, looking uncertain.

Theo's gaze was steady and observant, a quiet

pressure at the edge of my awareness. "Protocols provide structure, not limitation." The words came out more authentic than any scripted talking point. "Document your findings. Propose an alternative analytical approach. If it proves more effective, we adapt the protocol."

"Really? I can deviate?"

"Innovation requires deviation." I met her earnest gaze. "This algorithm evolves because everyone on this team pushes its boundaries, not just follows established paths."

As Alicia turned back to her work, energized, I understood how important the interaction was, and that Theo had been watching. I glanced at him, expecting a cynical comment about corporate empowerment talk.

Instead, his expression held warmth, an undeniable appreciation that unsettled me more than I wanted to admit.

"What?"

"Nothing." He shook his head, a small smile playing on his lips. "It's just different seeing you interact with your team. Less CEO, more mentor."

"Talent development is critical for maintaining our competitive edge." I adjusted my glasses, forcing myself not to take a moment to clean them so I could reset. "Investing in people optimizes long-term system performance."

"If you say so." Theo's tone suggested he heard the carefully constructed rationale but saw something else entirely.

"It's interesting you talked about deviation as innovation here, but in cooking class you hold tight to the recipe." He cocked his eyebrow as a smirk played at his lips.

Talking about the class threw me, but it occurred to me that he wasn't wrong about my different approaches. "That might be something to analyze at another time."

I directed him to the glass-walled conference room at the heart of the floor—my personal workspace within the dev center. Screens lined one wall, displaying real-time algorithm performance metrics and complex correlation matrices.

"This is where I work when I need to engage with the core system architecture and analyze nuanced patterns without distraction." I paused at the door a moment to acknowledge what it meant to let him in.

Theo moved toward a screen showing a swirling visualization of compatibility factors. "Relationship success indicators?"

"Simplified, but essentially yes." I stood beside

him, close enough to register the faint scent of his worn leather jacket. "We track thousands of interaction variables, mapping correlations with relationship satisfaction and longevity."

"But how do you define satisfaction?" He echoed our earlier debates but with a different tone now—less challenge, more inquiry. "Longevity doesn't always equal quality. Some brief connections are profoundly meaningful."

"That's a known limit of our current model. Our next version will include better measures for how deep relationships are and people's well-being, going beyond just how long they last."

Theo looked surprised. "You're acknowledging core limitations? Publicly?"

"Internally first," I clarified. "But yes. The algorithm evolves as our understanding evolves. Scientific integrity demands acknowledging what we don't yet know, or what we're still refining."

"That's not the impression LoveLogic projects to the public." He studied me, not the screens. "The marketing emphasizes certainty, predictive power."

"Marketing demands confidence. Science requires humility." I met his gaze. "My primary identity is scientist."

Something subtle recalibrated between us. The script was completely gone.

"May I?" Theo gestured to an auxiliary console.

I hesitated barely a second. "Go ahead."

He sat, navigating the interface with intuitive speed. "So these complementary patterns—you weight them more heavily than simple similarities for certain traits?"

"Correct." I leaned over his shoulder, pointing to a complex node map. "How people handle feelings, think about things, or deal with fights often works better when their differences fit well together. Our system is made to find those connections."

"Like your analytical precision and my intuitive leaps." Theo navigated deeper into the data.

His personal analogy caught me off guard. "That's an accurate representation of the principle, yes."

For the next hour, we discussed algorithm architecture, behavioral psychology, and the ethics of pattern recognition. Theo's questions were insightful, revealing a sophisticated understanding that went far beyond his published critiques.

"The main challenge," I explained, "is balancing group patterns with individual choice. How do we use data about populations to see potential without treating people like statistics?"

"A paradox." Theo leaned against the console, watching me intently. "Your system needs to categorize to match, but true connection often happens when people defy categorization."

"Exactly!" The word escaped with more enthusiasm than I'd intended. "Which is why we're developing adaptive prediction—systems that learn an individual's unique patterns and recognize constructive deviations from the norm."

Theo smiled. "You almost sound like a romantic, Mendez. Searching for the beautiful exception within the data."

"I'm a realist," I corrected. "Romance without compatibility is ephemeral. Compatibility without chemistry is functional but uninspired. The algorithm identifies the intersection where both might flourish."

The door chimed, breaking the spell. Trina entered, her eyes darting between us, the whiteboard, and the screens. No doubt she was considering how much I'd shown Theo.

"Apologies for interrupting," she said. "Zach, your investor call is in fifteen minutes."

I checked my watch, startled. I'd lost all track of time. "Thank you, Trina. We're just finishing."

She nodded, though her gaze lingered, registering the proximity. "I can escort Mr. Barrett out so you can prepare."

"That won't be necessary." Theo gathered his

notebook, his expression thoughtful. "I wasn't expecting this much insight. It was illuminating."

As we walked back toward the elevators, a reluctance slowed my steps. The tour had strayed from even the revised plan I'd created—yet somehow, it felt more productive.

"Thank you," Theo said as we waited, "for showing me beyond the polished facade."

"You would have seen through the facade anyway," I replied.

"Probably." He smiled faintly. "But I wouldn't have understood the intellectual passion driving it. Or the collaborative dynamic you foster."

The elevator arrived, its doors sliding open. We stepped inside.

"Will this visit alter your book's critique?" I adjusted my tone, aiming to reintroduce a layer of professional distance.

"Yes. It will definitely shape the analysis. Make it more detailed, more honest."

When we reached the lobby, I expected a formal goodbye. Instead, Theo turned to face me.

"The literary reading is in a few days," he said. "My turf this time."

"I'm aware of the schedule."

"Just..." He hesitated. "Approach it with the same openness you showed today."

I nodded, unable to trust my voice for a reply that wouldn't betray the confusing mix of professional caution and personal eagerness that rushed through me.

As he walked toward the exit, his stride confident, his presence lingering even after he'd disappeared through the revolving doors, Trina stepped in next to me.

"That was never approved for him to see." Her voice had a tinge of annoyance.

"No. It wasn't."

"Sharing proprietary algorithm insights with our most prominent critic involves significant corporate risk."

"He signed an NDA extensive enough to cover rogue nation-states." I turned toward the elevators.

Trina fell into step beside me. "This isn't just about NDAs, Zach, and you know it. You didn't only show him the dev center. You showed him you. The scientist behind the CEO. Was that the plan?"

I didn't respond.

"One question before your call," she said as we reached the elevator bank.

"What's that?"

"When I walked in and you were explaining the adaptive prediction models to him—did you realize you were smiling? A real, unguarded one." She pressed the 'up' button. "I haven't seen that expression since before LoveLogic existed." She touched my arm, her gaze gentle. "It was good to see."

The elevator doors opened, but I didn't step inside, caught by what her observation suggested.

Had I been smiling? Had my professional armor cracked so visibly? The possibility was unsettling—and, I had to admit, not unwelcome.

## 9

Theo

I sat cross-legged on my sofa, laptop balanced precariously on the armrest, the cursor blinking with mocking regularity. Notes from my visit to LoveLogic headquarters lay scattered around me—a chaotic collection of observations that refused to coalesce into what I needed to write.

Something still wasn't working.

I typed, deleted, typed again.

*Mendez, despite his company's rhetoric about connection, remained detached from the human element...*

Delete.

Detached? No. That wasn't right.

I pictured him in the algorithm development

center, leaning over that developer's shoulder. His focus hadn't been detached. It had been intense, almost protective.

Innovation requires deviation. That wasn't the soundbite of a detached CEO.

*LoveLogic's founder presented a meticulously polished image, deflecting substantive questions about ethical concerns...*

Zach hadn't deflected, not really. Instead, he'd admitted the limitations of their metrics, acknowledged the theatricality of the innovation lab versus the 'real work' happening upstairs. What he showed me wasn't just the packaging—it was the engine.

With a frustrated sigh, I slammed the laptop shut and pushed off the sofa. The energy of the dev center—the quiet hum, the focused intensity, the collaborative vibe—it clashed with the narrative I'd constructed for months.

Tech mogul treats human connection like debugging code. Cold. Analytical. Devoid of genuine human insight.

Except the man I'd spent hours with yesterday hadn't been cold.

Passionate when defending his creation? Yes.

Articulate in both its technological intricacies and its intended human benefits? Annoyingly so.

Willing to engage with ethical nuances beyond talking points? Unexpectedly, yes.

This complicated everything.

I paced the length of my living room, navigating the familiar obstacle course of overflowing bookshelves and vinyl record stacks.

Why was this so hard? He was the embodiment of everything I argued against. Why couldn't I articulate the dangers of his calculated approach to human connection?

Because the calculation now seemed intertwined with something harder to label. Conviction? Belief? Maybe even a strange sort of integrity within his own logical framework?

My phone rang, the sharp sound slicing through my thoughts.

Vivian. Perfect.

"Tell me you've got something incendiary from yesterday's tour," she said before I had a chance to say hello.

"I'm working on it." I moved to the window, watching raindrops trace slow patterns down the glass. "It's more complicated than I expected."

"Complicated how?" Suspicion sharpened her tone. "Did the tech temple disappoint? Not enough soulless drones in pods?"

"Something like that." I ran a hand over my face.

"Mendez isn't the detached technocrat I painted him as. There's substance there. Passion, even. It throws a wrench in the villain narrative."

A weighted pause. "Are you going soft on me? Need I remind you we have a deadline and a publisher expecting your signature critical take?"

"I'm being thorough. Good journalism means acknowledging complexity, not just confirming biases."

"Hmm." The sound conveyed volumes of editorial doubt. "Well, thorough or not, Audrey wants to meet tomorrow about the book's progress. Publisher's getting antsy with the moved-up timeline. They loved the buzz from the museum and cooking class, but they need pages."

"Already? We've only had two of the four scheduled dates."

"That's why they want an update now. To capitalize on the momentum." The distinct click of her keyboard punctuated her words. "The online narrative is gaining traction. People are eating up the dynamic between you two."

My stomach tightened at that dynamic—the intellectual sparring, the unexpected moments of connection.

"Meeting's at eleven," Vivian continued. "Bring whatever you have, even if it's *complicated*."

After hanging up, I stared out at the gray afternoon. The pressure of my to-do list mounted. Rewrite the article. Prepare for the meeting. Untangle the confusing knot of my reactions to Zach Mendez.

<hr>

WALKING into the meeting with Vivian and Audrey was like entering pressure cooker. Audrey, impeccable as always in a stylish suit, got straight to the point, bypassing pleasantries.

"The publisher loves the attention your *experiment* is getting." She gestured to her tablet, displaying social media analytics. "Engagement is through the roof. But they're concerned the manuscript isn't capitalizing on the core narrative."

"Which narrative is that?" I braced myself.

"The human story." Vivian leaned forward. "The dynamic between you and Mendez. Critic versus creator. Logic versus love—or whatever hashtag is trending this week. That's what readers are responding to." She swiped on the tablet, showing me photos—Zach and I at the museum, leaning in during debate. A shot from the cooking class where he was laughing, genuinely laughing, at something I'd said. "This chemistry, this friction—it's gold. But your latest pages barely touch on it."

"It's a professional arrangement." I shifted uncomfortably. "The dynamic is intellectual debate, not personal drama."

Audrey arched a sculpted eyebrow. "Perhaps. But the public perception is different. They see sparks. They see two brilliant minds colliding. That's the narrative driving interest. Your book needs to deliver on that promise."

"I'm writing a critique of algorithmic dating, not a romance novel." Frustration was building.

"And that critique is strongest when grounded in the human element," Vivian argued. "You need to show us Mendez, the man behind the algorithm. What drives him? What makes him believe he can quantify connection? Readers need that context to grasp your thesis."

"So dig deeper." Audrey's tone implied this was a simple directive. "Give us the personal angle. Understand his motivations, his background. That's where the real story lies—the one the publisher wants, and the one with the power to make this book compelling."

Their arguments were professionally sound, infuriatingly logical.

To properly critique LoveLogic, I needed to

understand its creator. But their focus came across as skewed, pushing the personal angle for commercial reasons rather than journalistic ones. And after yesterday, the thought of dissecting Zach's motivations was complicated. Invasive, almost.

"I'll consider how to incorporate more context." The concession felt like a compromise. "But I'm not turning this into a personality profile."

"Just give us the human story." She sensed her victory. "The man behind the code."

By the time I left the meeting, a headache pulsed at the edges of my vision and unease had taken root. The book I'd set out to write was slipping away, replaced by something shaped by public perception and publisher demands.

THAT EVENING, I bypassed the stalled article draft and opened a new browser window instead. If I needed to understand Zach's personal motivations to contextualize his work properly, I'd do it my way—research first, questions later.

I dug beyond the polished corporate profiles, searching academic databases, MIT archives, obscure tech blogs from LoveLogic's early days. Piece by careful piece, a different narrative began to emerge, one that chipped away further at the simplistic CEO caricature.

Working-class Chicago upbringing. Immigrant parents who sacrificed for his education. Scholarships won through sheer coding talent. The surprising double major—Computer Science and Psychology. Why psychology? What questions about the human mind drove the code?

His undergraduate thesis explored pattern recognition in relationship formation, blending behavioral psychology with computational analysis. An early paper, co-authored with a prominent attachment theorist, focused on quantifying behavioral markers —the foundational seeds of LoveLogic's compatibility metrics.

The man who had debated algorithmic ethics with such precision wasn't a product of Silicon Valley privilege. He'd built this in a dorm room, fueled by intellectual curiosity and, it seemed, a deep-seated interest in why human connections succeeded or failed. His empire was shaped by intellectual drive, not inherited advantage.

This didn't invalidate my critique. Good intentions could still pave the way to ethically questionable systems. But the simplistic villain narrative? It crumbled further, leaving behind a complex, contradictory figure who seemed driven by a genuine fascination with the very human complexities his critics accused him of ignoring.

What had happened in his life to make him so focused on predicting compatibility? Why the focus on psychology alongside the code? Why the painstakingly constructed professional armor I've glimpsed cracks in?

The research provided context but answered none of the core questions. The man remained an enigma, more complex and compelling than the *algorithm man* I'd initially set out to dismantle. And the uncomfortable truth settled in my gut: understanding Zach Mendez was no longer just a professional requirement for my book. It had become a personal imperative I couldn't ignore.

# 10

Zach

I scanned the crowded TechFuture launch event floor. Industry heavyweights, venture capitalists, journalists—a familiar sea of faces I usually navigated with precision. Tonight, though, my gaze kept drifting towards the entrance, an illogical anticipation tightening my chest.

Focus.

The presentation on our new compatibility visualization technology was about to begin. The stakes were high—investor confidence, competitive positioning, reinforcing our market leadership. This level of internal distraction was unlike me.

I forced my attention back to the talking points on my tablet, rereading the same bullet point three times without processing its content. Networking buzzed around me—conversation, the clink of glasses —it all faded against the internal pull towards... what, exactly?

The memory of Theo's curiosity during our office tour? The unexpected vulnerability he'd shared at that cafe?

"Mendez! Didn't expect to see you mingling with the commoners before your presentation."

I turned, pushing my thoughts of Theo aside.

Benjamin Bradford, founder of SoulSync—our less successful, spiritually-inclined competitor— approached, champagne flute already half-empty. Daria Novak, DatePotential's sharp-eyed CTO, and another executive I half-recognized flanked him.

"Benjamin." I extended a hand, the grip firm, the smile precisely calibrated. "Looking forward to your panel tomorrow."

"Should be entertaining." Benjamin smirked. "We've got that journalist on the panel—Barrett, the one who's been carving you up." He took a pointed sip of champagne. "Though I hear you've been handling him *personally*. Compatibility experiment, right?"

The slight emphasis on *personally* made my jaw tighten. "The initiative has provided valuable data."

"Valuable data?" Daria Novak's tone always cut

through pretense. "That's not what social media is saying. People are running betting pools on whether you'll end up proving your algorithm right or falling for the enemy."

Public speculation wasn't my concern. And Theo wasn't the enemy. "The data speaks for itself."

"Speaking of your pet critic." Benjamin leaned in with feigned conspiracy. "We were just discussing Barrett's latest diatribe. Guy's got a real technophobic crusade going. All that romantic nonsense about *authentic connection* being undermined by algorithms." He rolled his eyes. "As if drunken bar hookups led to better relationships than scientifically validated compatibility."

Irritation surged—sharp, unexpected, difficult to tamp down.

"Barrett's critique is more nuanced than that." The words emerging before my internal filter could catch them. I saw Benjamin and Daria exchange a quick, surprised glance.

"Come on, Mendez," Benjamin scoffed. "The guy called algorithmic matching 'emotional strip-mining.' He's a Luddite with a poetic vocabulary."

"He's questioning the ethics of our methodologies, not technology itself," I countered. "His concerns about data privacy and algorithmic transparency are legitimate points of discussion in our industry."

Why was I defending him? Understanding criticism was sound strategy, yes, but this was different.

Daria's eyes narrowed, sharp with calculation. "Sounds like you've been listening very closely to his critiques."

"I make a habit of understanding substantive criticism rather than dismissing it." My voice cooled, a layer of detachment settling over the earlier heat. "Barrett's journalistic process is thorough, even when I disagree with his conclusions."

Benjamin raised his bushy eyebrows, a knowing, unpleasant smile spreading across his face. "Defending the enemy now, Zach? That's a new look for you."

"He's not the enemy. He's a journalist." I glanced at my watch. "If you'll excuse me, I need to check in with my team before the presentation."

I turned away, catching their exchanged glances before moving through the crowd. Defending Theo seemed strange to them. Was my objectivity compromised?

Trina stood near the stage, coordinating with the event staff. "Everything's set." Her gaze was sharp as I approached. "Slides loaded, demo tested. The visualization looks spectacular on the big screen."

"Good." I scanned the audience, a conditioned reflex, though I knew who I was looking for. "Media attendance confirmed?"

"Mr. Barrett arrived ten minutes ago. In the back, left side."

I followed her line of sight, over rows of expectant faces, until I saw him. Theo. He stood slightly apart, notebook in hand, that always-untamed salt-and-pepper hair impossible to miss. He wore a dark blazer over a vintage Culture Club tee—defying the corporate dress code while radiating an intensity that drew the eye.

"You should probably stop staring." Trina's voice was dry. "Benjamin Bradford is probably already gossiping."

"I wasn't staring."

"Of course you weren't." Her tone was skeptical. "Presentation starts in fifteen. You should head backstage."

The quiet backstage area offered a brief reprieve. I reviewed my notes one last time, the technical details of the new visualization interface solidifying in my mind. This feature represented a step towards user empowerment, allowing individuals to explore the multi-dimensional nature of compatibility beyond a single percentage.

It addressed, indirectly, some of Theo's *black box* criticisms. Would he see it that way?

When my name was announced, I stepped onto the stage. I found my mark, adjusted the microphone, and began with practiced confidence, outlining LoveLogic's commitment to evolving alongside user needs.

Three minutes in, my attention drifted to the back left. Theo sat attentive, pen moving across his notebook. I felt a distinct pull—a subconscious urge to deviate from the script, to address the human element more directly than planned.

Throughout the presentation, I made micro-adjustments to my remarks—subtly emphasizing user agency, acknowledging algorithmic limitations alongside strengths, highlighting the collaborative effort behind the technology. Each time I registered Theo's presence, a silent audience of one whose critique spurred me toward greater authenticity in my corporate messaging.

The Q&A followed. Hands went up—developers with technical queries, journalists seeking competitive angles. I fielded them all with my usual precision. But Theo didn't raise his hand.

He watched, listened, made notes. Was he absorbing? Critiquing internally? Saving his fire for later?

After the presentation concluded, the stage became a vortex of congratulations and follow-up questions from investors and industry colleagues. I navigated the interactions with efficiency, shaking hands, reinforcing key messages. Through gaps in the crowd, I saw Theo still observing from the edge of the room, his perceptive gaze taking everything in.

I managed to extract myself from a prolonged discussion with an enthusiastic venture capitalist. I made my way to the relative quiet of the refreshment area and spotted Theo as he finished a conversation with another reporter near the exit. An impulse, illogical and immediate, took hold.

I approached just as the other journalist walked away. "Barrett." I defaulted to formality in this public sphere. "I'm surprised you didn't speak up during the presentation."

He turned, that familiar half-smile tilting his lips. "I have plenty of questions, Mendez. Just not ones suited for that particular forum."

"Professional questions, or personal?" The words slipped out, pushing a boundary I hadn't intended to test.

"Both, actually."

A beat of silence stretched between us. For the first time in years, navigating a professional interaction left me uncertain. What were the parameters now?

"There's a whiskey bar around the corner," I said before I could overthink it. It was quieter. More conducive to nuanced questions. "If you're interested."

Theo studied me, surprise clear in his expression, followed by that curiosity I admired. "Are you suggesting an unscheduled, off-the-record extension of our arrangement?"

"I'm suggesting a conversation in a setting more appropriate for substantive discussion than this." I gestured at the crowded room, even as I knew my motivation was simpler. I wanted more time with him, away from the performance. "Unless you have other commitments."

He considered this, his gaze steady on mine. "Lead the way."

I sent Trina a brief text about my departure, ignoring her immediate *With Barrett?* reply. We slipped out a side entrance, the relative quiet of the street a welcome change.

The whiskey bar was a cocoon of dark wood, low lighting, and soft jazz—an atmosphere designed for contemplation rather than networking. We found a corner booth, the worn leather sighing faintly as we settled opposite each other. After ordering—single malt for me, something complex involving rye for him—a new silence fell, charged with unspoken questions.

"Your presentation was different from what I expected."

"Different how?" I was genuinely curious.

"More focused on user understanding, less on algorithmic superiority. Almost as if you were consciously addressing some of the ethical concerns I've raised."

Our drinks arrived and I took a deliberate sip of whiskey, the peaty warmth of comfort.

Should I acknowledge his influence? Maintain professional distance? The truth was risky to admit.

"Perhaps your critiques have influenced our development priorities," I admitted.

"Have they?"

"Good science requires considering alternative perspectives." My familiar rationale seemed less like a shield than ever before. "Even those that fundamentally question your approach."

Theo leaned back. "Did you just admit that my technophobic crusade has merit?"

"I conceded your questions have value," I clarified. "Even when your conclusions are demonstrably flawed."

"And earlier?" His smile faded slightly, replaced

by a questioning look. "When you defended me to your competitors? Was that also acknowledging my questions have value?"

I froze, my glass halfway to my lips. "You heard that?"

"I was nearby." His gaze was unwavering.

A flush of heat rose in my face. "I merely corrected an oversimplification of your published position."

"You called my journalistic process thorough." His eyes were bright with something I couldn't quite decipher. "That's practically a love letter in tech CEO language."

"Professional respect isn't unusual between intellectual adversaries."

"Is that what we are?" Theo's voice dropped. "Adversaries?"

The question landed, cutting through layers of pretense.

What were we? Experiment participants? Reluctant collaborators?

A connection that defied categorization?

"I don't know anymore," I admitted.

Theo leaned forward, his journalistic instincts replaced by something more personal. "Why did you create LoveLogic, Zach? Not the official founder's story, the one polished for investors. The real reason."

The question probed the core motivation, the vulnerability I never discussed. I took another sip of whiskey, the liquid fire doing little to quell the sudden internal chill. This was territory I never shared.

Yet, looking at Theo across the small table, I saw curiosity in his eyes, without a trace of journalistic calculation. A quiet urge to explain overtook me.

To be understood beyond the algorithm.

"Efficiency wasn't the only motivation." I measured each word, deciding how much to reveal. "Though that's the narrative that resonated most effectively with early funding rounds."

"What was the other motivation?" he prompted gently.

I traced the condensation ring my glass left on the dark wood, avoiding his direct gaze. The admission was like shedding armor piece by piece. "Prevention."

"Prevention of what?"

"Mismatched connections." The words felt inadequate. "Relationships built on incomplete information. Assumptions." I paused, then forced myself to continue. "The pain that comes from believing you know someone intimately, when in reality, you never really knew them at all."

Theo waited, his silence more effective than any probing question.

The memories surfaced with unwelcome clarity. "Seven years ago, I was working on the early algorithm concepts. I was... involved with someone. Marco. He seemed to understand my work, my ambitions. Supported me." My voice tightened. "We were together for almost a year."

"What happened?" Theo asked softly.

The details still cut deep. "He was gathering information for a competitor. Not just about the algorithm—though he took early code, research notes—but personal details. Vulnerabilities. Things I'd shared believing we had intimacy."

The confession hung in the air. Saying it out loud was like exposing a critical system flaw. I braced for judgment, for analysis.

Theo's expression wasn't journalistic or analytical. "I'm sorry that happened to you, Zach."

I retreated instinctively to my usual framework. "I learned a valuable lesson in data security protocols and the importance of compartmentalization."

"No." Theo cut through my deflection. "It was a betrayal of trust. A violation. Not a lesson in security protocols."

His direct naming of the emotional reality—the one I'd spent years reframing through a lens of logic and professional consequence—jolted me. He saw the personal wound beneath the corporate scar tissue.

"Perhaps it was both," I conceded.

A wave of panic hit me—I'd revealed too much, strayed too far from the controlled narrative. This wasn't a good idea. "This isn't relevant to your research." I pulled back, reasserting boundaries.

"I wasn't asking as a journalist." His gaze held mine, acknowledging the shift that had occurred between us.

We had crossed a line, moved from professional arrangement to something undeniably personal.

"I should go." I reached for my jacket, needing to restore distance, regain control. "Early meetings tomorrow."

Theo didn't argue, didn't push. But his expression held a quiet understanding that I was retreating—not from him, but from what I'd revealed.

"Thank you for the insight into your visualization technology." He allowed me the professional exit strategy. "It's an interesting step toward the transparency I've been advocating for."

"I look forward to reading your perspective on

it." My tension eased as the conversation shifted back to safer ground.

We walked out together into the cool night air. My driver idled down the street.

"My car's waiting."

"I'll walk," Theo said.

An impulse surfaced—offer him a ride. I suppressed it. Compartmentalization was key.

"Goodnight, Zach." His eyes lingered on mine a beat longer than necessary. "Thanks for defending my journalistic integrity today."

"I merely stated facts."

His smile suggested he saw right through it. "Right. Facts."

As my car pulled away, I watched him recede in the side mirror—that confident stride, the defiant casualness in every step.

I had defended him. Adjusted my presentation for him. Invited him for off-the-record drinks. Shared the Marco story—a piece of history I guarded obsessively.

I stared out at the city lights and had to admit—with a startling lack of my usual analytical detachment—that I didn't regret a single deviation.

# 11

Theo

ZACH'S CAR PULLED AWAY, its taillights reflecting red streaks on the wet pavement before vanishing around the corner. I stood there on the sidewalk, the cool night air damp against my skin.

Something remained unfinished. Like a conversation paused mid-sentence, the most crucial part still unspoken.

That admission about Marco had done more than make Zach's CEO mask slip—it cracked it wide open. For a moment, I saw the man underneath. The one who'd been wounded years ago and had built a fortress of logic and control to protect himself. He'd retreated almost instantly, but I'd seen it.

Seen him.

Rain began to fall again, a persistent, misty drizzle that beaded on my leather jacket. Streetlights haloed in the damp air. I should start walking. Head home. Process. Write.

Instead, I pulled out my phone, the screen bright against the dark street. Zach's contact info sat there, added weeks ago during contract negotiations.

No cameras. No publicity angle. No research justification. Just an impulse. An unwillingness to let the night end on that note of hesitant retreat.

My thumb hovered over the message icon. What was I even doing?

Screw it.

Theo: *That whiskey deserved more than one round.*

Message sent. Too late to reconsider. The blue bubble sat there, stark against the white background. Almost immediately, the three dots appeared.

Zach: *My car passed a 24-hour diner two blocks back. Apparently makes excellent pie.*

I let out a breath, a small smile pulling at my lips despite myself.

Theo: *Pie trumps whiskey after 10 PM. It's a scientific fact.*

Zach: *I'd need to see the research validating that claim.*

I started walking in the direction his car had gone.

Theo: *I'll cite my sources over coffee. Turn your car around.*

Three minutes later, dripping slightly, I spotted his car pulled up beside a beacon of unlikely retro charm. Chrome gleamed under the blue neon sign: *Sunny's.* It looked like a movie set dropped onto the darkened street.

Zach stood beneath the diner's small, striped awning, looking out of place and yet perfectly composed in his expensive suit amid the flickering neon. He'd removed his tie, stuffing it into a pocket, and a few raindrops clung to his dark hair.

"Decided the night wasn't over?" I stepped beside him, shaking rain from my jacket.

"I decided I was hungry." The corner of his mouth twitched upward. "And your claim about pie required immediate investigation."

Inside Sunny's Diner there was the aroma of coffee and frying onions, and the low murmur of conversation. A waitress with vibrant purple hair and tired eyes waved us toward a row of empty booths along the window.

We slid onto cracked red vinyl seats opposite each other. The laminated menu displayed photos of dishes that looked like they belonged in the 1980s.

"Not my usual dining spot." Zach surveyed the scene with undisguised curiosity.

"Why not?" I countered. "Is it the vintage ketchup dispensers or the distinct lack of polished concrete?"

"The probability of encountering venture capitalists is statistically negligible here. So, it has that going for it."

"Exactly." I grinned, setting the menu down as the purple-haired waitress ambled over, notepad ready. "Some decisions should remain blissfully unoptimized."

We ordered coffee and pie—apple for me, blueberry for him.

"You didn't have to turn your car around."

Zach traced the condensation ring his water glass left on the Formica tabletop, his gaze focused on the movement. Processing. "You didn't have to text me."

"Fair point." I leaned back against the vinyl seat. "Why did you decide to meet?"

He looked up then, his dark eyes meeting mine across the table. The fluorescent lights reflected in his glasses, momentarily obscuring his expression. "I wasn't finished talking to you." The directness caught me off guard. "That's the simple truth."

Before I could process that admission, our waitress

returned, sliding large white mugs of coffee and plates bearing enormous wedges of pie onto the table. The smell of cinnamon and baked apples filled the air.

"So." I began again after she left, picking up my fork. "Marco."

Zach froze, his fork halfway to his slice of blueberry pie. The ease that had settled between us vanished, replaced by a familiar guardedness. "I shouldn't have mentioned him."

"Why not?" My journalist instincts warred with personal feelings. I wanted clarity for myself, not just for the book.

"Because it's not relevant."

I set my fork down. This wasn't about relevance. It was about trust.

"I'm not asking as a journalist right now, Zach. I'm asking as..." I paused, the words catching in my throat. What were we? Adversaries? Collaborators? "As someone who wants to know you better. Off the record. No notes. Only conversation."

He studied me for a long moment. I saw the internal calculation—risk assessment versus the potential benefit of sharing his story. I held his gaze, trying my best to convey sincerity beyond words. Something seemed to shift behind his eyes. He set his fork down beside his untouched pie and took a slow breath, the kind one takes before diving into deep water.

"Marco was my first serious relationship." His voice was quieter now, missing some of its usual precise cadence. "We met my final year at MIT. I was focused on the early algorithm concepts. Barely slept. Lived on caffeine, soup, and code." He offered a small, self-deprecating smile. "He was charismatic. Interested in my work. Made me feel seen when I felt mostly invisible—just the scholarship kid obsessed with computational patterns."

I nodded, picturing a younger, less armored Zach.

"I shared everything with him." His gaze dropped back to the table. "Not just the technical details—though I gave those freely—but my ambitions. My belief that I could help people avoid unnecessary relational pain." His voice tightened. "I even introduced him to my family. My abuela."

The mention of his grandmother, who he'd spoken of with such warmth during the cooking class, underscored the depth of the betrayal.

"Eight months in, I found emails." He picked up his fork and poked at the crust. "Correspondence with his actual employer—DateSync. They were one of our earliest competitors." The words were clipped, and emotion controlled. "He'd been feeding them everything. Code snippets. Research directions. Even personal details I'd shared in confidence."

"Jesus, Zach." The crudeness escaped before I could stop it. This was more than corporate espionage. "That's..."

"A comprehensive violation." His voice was devoid of inflection. "Personal and professional boundaries breached with calculated intent."

The pieces clicked into place with sudden clarity. His rigid boundaries. His reluctance to use his own platform. His almost obsessive focus on control and data security. It wasn't just about building a company. It was about building defenses.

"The betrayal wasn't only the stolen work." I understood how deeply he'd been wounded.

Zach looked up, surprise flickering across his features, followed by... relief? "Exactly. Most people focus on the intellectual property theft. The financial implications." He met my eyes. "Few grasp the personal pain."

"Is that why?" I hesitated, unsure if I was crossing a line. "Is that why you haven't dated since? Why you built a system for others but kept yourself outside it?"

He raised an eyebrow, a spark of the familiar

intellectual challenge returning. "You've been researching my personal history?"

"Basic background," I admitted. "Sparse details. You guard your privacy well."

"Not well enough." A ghost of a smile touched his lips. "To answer your question, yes. After Marco, personal relationships seemed an unacceptable risk. Building LoveLogic required complete focus."

"So you developed an algorithm to predict compatibility, partly as a shield against repeating that kind of betrayal."

"The algorithm was an attempt to bring structure to chaos. To help people identify genuine compatibility before emotional investment clouds judgment. Before vulnerability becomes a liability."

He shared his painful history, trusting me enough to offer the reason behind the walls he'd put in place.

We sat in silence for a moment, the only sound the clatter of dishes from the kitchen. There was a fragile, genuine quality to what he'd shared.

"You know, thinking about the story you told me about your parents' separation," Zach said finally. "It seems our motivations aren't as diametrically opposed as they appear on the surface. You critique systems for their potential to dehumanize connection. I built one attempting to protect people from the pain of failed connection."

"Different responses to the same underlying fear," I acknowledged. "That human connection is delicate, easy to break, whether by betrayal or by spreadsheet."

He nodded. "The problem isn't the algorithms, not really. We want easy answers and certainty, even when things are naturally uncertain."

This wasn't a debate about technology versus humanity anymore. We were discussing the human needs and vulnerabilities that both drove technological development and shaped our responses to it.

The waitress kept our coffee cups filled. The diner had emptied further, but we kept talking.

"Do you ever wonder if your experience with Marco made you overly reliant on systems and data? As a way to avoid the messiness of trust?"

"I've considered it." His gaze stayed steady on mine. "It's more efficient to analyze data than navigate emotional uncertainty. Safer." He looked down at his hands resting on the table. "Though perhaps at a cost I've only recently begun to realize."

The honesty of his admission resonated. This wasn't a detached CEO. It was someone grappling with the limitations of his own tightly constructed world.

"For what it's worth, I think what you made with LoveLogic has probably helped many people." I wanted to offer something beyond critique. "My issue isn't that these systems have no value. It's the promise of certainty. The implication that connection can be optimized, guaranteed."

"That's more nuanced than your published articles suggest."

"My perspective is evolving," I admitted. "Some of my initial assumptions have been challenged."

"By what?"

"By whom," I corrected.

The waitress appeared with the check, placing it between us. Zach reached for it without hesitation.

"My half," I protested.

"Consider it continued empirical investigation." That slight smile returned. "I'm curious. What would you call this?"

This.

I thought about the whiskey bar, this late-night diner confession. "I don't know anymore. But it's not just research."

"No," he agreed. "It's not."

We walked out into the cool, clean air of the post-rain city. Zach's driver waited at the curb.

"My car." He gestured.

"I'll walk. Need to clear my head."

We stood facing each other on the sidewalk, the blue neon of Sunny's casting shadows on his face. That lingering intimacy from our conversation created a space apart from the surrounding city.

"The literary reading is tomorrow night." The reminder of our structured arrangement seemed out-of-place.

"I've been preparing," he replied. "I downloaded several poetry collections to analyze recurring thematic structures."

I laughed. "Of course you did. You're always trying to optimize your emotional response through data analysis."

"Attempting to understand the appeal," he corrected, but his eyes held warmth.

"Some things are meant to be experienced, not analyzed." After everything we'd shared, the words carrying double meaning now.

"Perhaps that's something I need to explore further."

The implication hung in the air between us. A pull, undeniable and unexpected, urged me closer. I resisted, reminding myself of blurred lines and professional ethics.

"Goodnight, Zach." I took a small step back, creating the necessary distance.

"Goodnight, Theo."

We looked at each other until he gave a nod and turned toward the car. I watched him go. Our shared vulnerability lingered as his car disappeared into the night.

# 12

Zach

THE PRODUCT TEAM meeting was already in progress when I arrived, the hum of discussion filling the glass-walled room. Slides detailing user engagement metrics glowed on the main screen. I took my place at the head of the table, connecting my laptop, a strange sense of detachment settling over me.

My mind kept overlaying crisp data points with the memory of how easily conversation had flowed with Theo in that brightly lit diner.

"Morning." I pulled up my presentation. "Today we're reviewing priorities for the Q3 system update."

I moved through the standard metrics—efficiency improvements, integration protocols, market responsiveness. My voice was steady, my delivery precise.

Autopilot. But beneath the surface, the aftershocks of last night still reverberated.

I paused for a moment before going to the next slide, bracing for its impact. "Our third priority will be enhancing algorithmic transparency."

A subtle shift in the room's energy. Riley straightened in his seat, his usual nervous energy focusing into keen interest.

"We've received consistent feedback that users desire more insight into the *why* behind their matches," I continued, laying out the sound rationale.

But this wasn't only user input—it was Theo's voice echoing my thoughts. His critiques pushed me toward an openness I hadn't prioritized before. "We need to provide tools that empower people to understand the compatibility factors at play, fostering trust through clarity."

"Like addressing the black box criticism?" Riley leaned forward.

"Exactly." I noticed a few surprised glances exchanged between product managers. This wasn't a radical departure, but it was a shift in emphasis, one driven by forces beyond market data.

The meeting continued, but it was less compelling than the memory of Theo's challenging questions that forced me to re-examine the system I'd built.

After we wrapped up, Riley lingered.

"The transparency initiative is brilliant." His enthusiasm eclipsed his usual deference. "It parallels some findings I've been analyzing from the publicity experiment data."

"What did you discover?"

He glanced around the now-empty room before continuing. "The compatibility factors between you and Mr. Barrett." He hesitated. "They're showing real-time validation through your interaction patterns. It's fascinating."

"Meaning?" My voice betrayed none of my sudden unease.

"The complementary communication styles the algorithm predicted. The behaviors are manifesting precisely as modeled." Excitement lit his eyes. "Your text exchanges exhibit the precise balance of challenge and support that the compatibility metrics identified. It's like watching the algorithm's predictions unfold in real time."

My hand moved instinctively toward my phone pocket. An illogical sense of violation that our private interactions, however mundane, had become data points.

"You've been analyzing our text messages?" The question came out sharp.

"Not the content," Riley clarified as color rose in

his cheeks. "Just the metadata—timing patterns, response lengths, conversation sustainability. All within the parameters of the research agreement."

Logically, it was acceptable. Part of the experiment. Yet the explanation barely soothed the sting of exposure.

"The results provide compelling validation for the model." Riley pressed on, oblivious to my turmoil.

"I'd like to see the compatibility data again." My request was driven by something other than scientific verification. A need to examine the information, to reconcile the algorithm's cold logic with the warmth I felt remembering Theo's messages. "The complete analysis, not just the summary metrics."

Riley's eyes widened slightly behind his glasses. "Of course. I can pull up the full dataset this afternoon."

---

Hours later, alone in my office, the city lights beginning to prick the twilight sky, I stared at the complete compatibility analysis between Theo and me.

*Complementary Cognitive Frameworks.*
*Shared Core Values (Integrity, Authenticity).*

*Adaptive Communication Potential.*

The algorithm's detached assessment mapped onto the messy reality of our interactions with startling accuracy. There were intense debates. Unexpected moments of shared understanding. Confessions over food and drinks. My scientific mind acknowledged the elegant proof of concept. But another part of me—one I was still learning to navigate—felt dissected.

Did the data explain the warmth that spread through my chest when Theo teased me? Did it quantify the comfort I'd had sharing the Marco story? Or did it simply reduce something complex and human to predictable patterns?

I traced a cluster representing "Constructive Tension" on the display. *That* phrase sounded too clinical for the sharp, stimulating energy of arguing with Theo.

A soft knock interrupted my thoughts. Trina stood in the doorway, her expression shrewd as she took in the multi-screen visualization.

"Riley mentioned you've been going over the compatibility data for a few hours." She entered and closed the door behind her. "Everything okay?"

"Just verifying the pattern recognition metrics." That justification sounded flimsy.

"Uh-huh." She sank into the chair opposite me,

her gaze unwavering. "And does this verification require the kind of intensity I'm seeing right now? You look like you're trying to debug the human condition."

"Ensuring algorithmic integrity is our focus, especially with the new updates pending." My posture remained stiff, hands automatically adjusting the position of my keyboard.

"Zach, I've known you since before LoveLogic existed." Trina's tone was both warm and concerned. "I've never seen you this invested in a compatibility analysis—not even when we were validating the core algorithm."

I started to formulate another professional justification, then stopped. Trina deserved better.

"The system identified patterns I didn't recognize." I hadn't admitted this to anyone. "It's... unsettling."

"Because it suggests your algorithm works in ways you didn't anticipate?"

"Because it suggests I'm not as objective about this experiment as I should be."

There. The truth, at last. A realization that the walls I'd built between logic and emotion were starting to crumble.

Trina studied me for a long moment, her expression softening further. "Would it be so terrible if your algorithm matched you with someone you actually connect with?"

"It complicates the publicity arrangement."

"Or maybe it validates everything you've been building for the past six years."

I removed my glasses, rubbing my eyes, the emotional toll of the day catching up with me. "The reading is tomorrow night."

"Yes." Even though we were back to business, Trina's voice indicated she wasn't fully back in CMO mode. "The PR team has the standard briefing prepared. Talking points, suggested interactions—"

"I don't want them," I interrupted, the decision crystallizing as I spoke. "Let's cancel the prep session."

Trina's eyebrows rose. "That's a significant departure from the plan."

"I think you'd agree that the plan hasn't been particularly effective so far." I grabbed a cleaning cloth from the drawer and wiped my lenses.

"The script undermines authentic interaction." I replaced my glasses. "It defeats the purpose of the compatibility assessment."

I also wanted to approach the next encounter with honesty, free of pretense or predetermined strategy. A step towards personal transparency, mirroring the professional one I'd advocated for earlier.

A small smile played at the corners of her mouth. "Very scientific rationale. Nothing to do with wanting to engage with Theo Barrett as a person rather than a publicity obligation?"

"The experiment benefits from authentic engagement."

"Of course." She stood, moving toward the door. "Just one thing to consider, Zach."

"What's that?"

"If the algorithm is right—if you and Theo really have the complementary traits it identified—then the *experiment* has already yielded its result." She paused, looking at me. "The only question is whether you're willing to accept it."

After she left, her words continued to echo in my head. I turned back to the compatibility data, but my focus shifted. Instead, I opened my text conversation with Theo, scrolling through our exchanges.

The evolution was undeniable—increasing message frequency, lengthening responses, growing personal disclosure. The algorithm had predicted this engagement trajectory.

But the data couldn't capture the anticipation that my heart sped up when his name appeared on my screen. The way his unexpected humor could make me smile, disrupting my composure.

My phone buzzed. A new message. Theo. As if he knew I was thinking about him.

Theo: *Fair warning about tomorrow. Poetry readings involve feelings expressed without statistical validation. May induce discomfort for algorithm enthusiasts.*

I smiled. My fingers moved across the keyboard.

Zach: *I've been preparing.*

Theo: *So you've said. Missing the entire point is very on-brand.*

Zach: *Just establishing a contextual framework for the evening.*

Theo: *The rational approach to poetry is precisely why you need this experience. 7pm, remember. Leave the spreadsheets at home.*

13

Theo

I PACED near the entrance of Bookmark Haven, a restless energy humming beneath my skin.

Inside, the labyrinth of well-loved shelves created intimate corridors, the back corner transformed into a small reading space with mismatched chairs and floor cushions bathed in a soft, inviting light. My literary sanctuary wasn't the same tonight. Its familiar comfort was overshadowed by the anticipation charging through me.

I checked my watch again. 6:52 PM.

He'll be here, I told myself.

I tried to center my thoughts—remind myself that this was part of the story I was documenting. That objectivity still mattered. But I wasn't sure I believed that anymore. Not when I'd spent way too long choosing an outfit that said *thoughtfully casual.*

I checked my reflection in the store's window and smoothed the simple button-down I wore under my jacket for the tenth time. I did my best not to look like I'd overthought it. Which, embarrassingly, I absolutely had.

A black car, incongruous on this quiet street, pulled up. Zach stepped out, and the sight of him sent another jolt through me. No suit, no tie. He dressed casually, like he had for the cooking class—dark rinse jeans, a dark blue Henley beneath the same blazer I'd seen before. His hair lacked its usual precise styling, falling more naturally. It made him seem less like the algorithm architect and more approachable.

It was disarming.

A couple of soft clicks sounded as a single photographer snapped images. I'd convinced Vivian that given the nature of the event, our full teams shouldn't be present. She and Trina agreed to a single, discreet photographer.

"You made it." I cringed at how inanely obvious it sounded.

"I'm punctual by nature." His smile was small, contained, but came across as genuine and not a performative act. "Plus, I was informed that arriving late to poetry readings is considered philistine behavior."

"Who told you that?" I smiled.

"The internet. I researched literary event etiquette."

The admission showed his vulnerability—a desire to navigate unfamiliar territory the right way, paired with his instinct to rely on research. It stirred something warm in my chest, pushing past the professional boundaries I kept trying to reinforce.

"Well, the internet was right for once." I nodded toward the cozy glow of the bookstore door. "Shall we?"

Inside, there was quiet conversation and the comforting smell of aging books. About thirty people had gathered, many who I recognized from previous readings. The staging area was simple—a single microphone stand, a stool, soft light.

"This is... not what I expected," Zach murmured as we found seats in the second row. His shoulder brushed mine as he sat.

"What were you expecting?" I was acutely aware of his proximity.

"Something more formal. Auditorium seating. Proper lighting." His eyes, sharp and analytical scanned the mismatched furniture, the shelves overflowing with books, the fairy lights strung overhead. "This feels like someone's living room."

"That's exactly the appeal." I watched him process the *inefficiency* of the setup. Yet, he didn't seem dismissive, more intrigued. "Poetry isn't meant to be sterile."

His gaze shifted to me then, direct and questioning. "What should I listen for? Theme development? Structural patterns? Recurring motifs?"

"Just feel it." I knew the words didn't give Zach what he needed.

Could the man who saw the world in data points experience something without dissecting it? A part of me hoped he could.

A slight crease appeared between his eyebrows, the familiar concentration settling onto his features as if I'd presented him with a challenging problem. Before he could respond, Marjorie, the bookstore owner with bright pink hair and perpetually ink-stained fingers, approached the microphone and welcomed everyone.

The first poet was a woman in her sixties, silver hair escaping a loose bun, hands moving like birds as she spoke of lost love and strength reclaimed through seasons. I watched Zach from the corner of my eye. His posture remained perfect, analytical attention evident. But then, something shifted. His focus deepened, a stillness settling over him that wasn't just politeness. He was listening, intently listening.

When she finished, the applause filled the small space. Zach joined in, his clapping measured but definite. "That was remarkable." He leaned closer, keeping his voice low. "The precision of her verse structure contrasted with the emotional rawness of the content."

A smile spread across my face. "You couldn't resist analyzing, could you?"

"I'm trying to experience and analyze simultaneously." There was a hint of defensiveness in his tone. "Is that not permissible?"

Three more poets followed, their voices weaving tales of city landscapes, political outrage, quiet domestic moments.

Zach leaned in more with each reading, his absorption complete. During a sharp piece about technological disconnection isolating modern lives, his hand brushed mine. The contact was brief, but electric. A current shot up my arm. I didn't pull away. He didn't either.

My mind raced—was this intentional? Unconscious? Did it mean anything?

The final reader was Colin, a young barista whose work always gut-punched me with its raw honesty. Tonight, he read about his father's rapid decline into dementia. He wove together stark descriptions of neurological decay with fragmented memories of their shared moments—clinical terms for dying brain pathways in the same breath as birthday celebrations already blurred by time.

When Colin finished, his voice overflowing with emotion, the room fell into a profound, almost breathless silence before erupting in applause. I turned to Zach, expecting a comment on structural integrity or thematic development. Instead, he was still, his gaze fixed on the now-empty stool, his usual composure momentarily fractured. I saw it—something deep and unguarded in his eyes, a slight tension in his jaw. He wasn't analyzing. He was feeling.

"That last one," he said softly, his voice rougher than I'd heard it before. "About the father—his ability to frame deterioration and memory as both scientific process and emotional experience..." He trailed off, searching for the words.

"Bridging your world and mine." The observation escaped before I could overthink it.

"Yes. Exactly that."

Marjorie announced a brief break before the open mic, and the spell snapped. We stood, the movement clumsy, navigating the small space toward the refreshment table where paper cups of cheap red wine waited.

I handed him a cup. I needed to restore some semblance of our usual dynamic. "Has this experience altered your position on the value of artistic expression?"

"You're asking if poetry has converted me from data to feelings in one evening?" His mouth quirked up at the corner. "Not entirely. But I'm recalibrating my assessment."

"That might be the most romantic thing an algorithm designer could possibly say." The words were out before I could stop them.

He laughed in a way I'd never heard from him. It wasn't a controlled CEO chuckle, but something rich that sent flutters through my chest in response. "I contain multitudes, Barrett."

My breath caught. "Did you just quote Walt Whitman to me?"

"I told you I prepared." He took a sip of wine. The intensity was back, but not adversarial. "Though I may have misinterpreted some of the material. Poetry isn't as straightforward as code."

"That's what makes it worth experiencing." An idea sparked, reckless and immediate. I gestured toward the door. "Want some air before the next section?"

We slipped outside into the cool night. The sky was clear and the stars were surprisingly visible between the city buildings.

"Thank you for this," Zach said after we'd walked half a block in a companionable silence. "It's not an experience I would have sought out on my own."

"That's the problem with algorithms," I replied, unable to resist. "They recommend more of what we already know we like, not what might move us in ways we don't anticipate."

"Though we're developing models that introduce controlled variability. Serendipity algorithms designed to address that limitation."

I stopped walking, turning to face him under the glow of a streetlamp. "Do you ever stop thinking like a programmer? Even for a second?"

"Do you ever stop thinking like a writer?" He matched my stance, the space between us suddenly charged. The air crackled with more than just the cool breeze.

"Fair point. But there's a difference between observing the world through words and trying to optimize it through code."

His expression softened, the usual defensiveness absent. "Is there? Both are attempts to make sense of human experience. To find patterns in chaos."

The insight caught me off guard.

An impulse hit, fueled by the wine, the poetry, the deepening connection. Professional boundaries seemed irrelevant. "I have something I want to show you." The words rushed out. "At my apartment."

His eyebrows lifted slightly, questioning.

"A book," I clarified. Heat rose in my face. "Related to what you said about patterns and meaning. It's a short walk, only a few blocks from here."

He hesitated, just for a moment, before a decision settled in his features. "Lead the way."

The walk to my building took barely any time at all.

"This is me." I stopped before my brownstone, which had more character than polish.

The reality hit me—I was inviting Zach Mendez, CEO of LoveLogic, subject of my critique, into my personal, decidedly unoptimized space.

"It's a bit chaotic," I warned as I fumbled with my keys. "Nothing like your minimalist penthouse, I imagine."

"You imagine my apartment often?" The teasing note in his voice was ridiculously charming.

"Only in service of character development for my book."

I unlocked the door.

My apartment. Familiar, comfortable disorder—

books stacked high, vintage movie posters on the wall, vinyl filling shelves. I watched Zach take it all in, self-conscious, seeing my beloved chaos through his ordered eyes.

"This is..." His gaze swept the room with analytical curiosity.

"A mess?" I offered, bracing for judgment.

"Curated chaos," he corrected. He moved toward the overflowing bookshelves near my desk, running a finger along a spine. "Everything has a purpose, just not a conventional organization system."

"That might be the nicest way anyone's ever described my place." I turned to the shelves myself, searching for the specific volume. "The book I wanted to show you is here somewhere."

While I scanned titles, Zach wandered toward my record collection, picking up albums, examining covers. "Do you organize your music by feeling rather than artist or genre?"

I looked up, startled. "How could you possibly know that?"

"The groupings defy conventional categorization, but there's clear intentionality." He turned, holding up two records—The Smiths and Etta James. "These are vastly different genres but share a certain melancholy optimism. A vibe."

"Most people think I just don't know the alphabet," I admitted as my voice caught.

"You're too precise with your book arrangement for that theory to hold." He replaced the albums. "Your organization is subjective, but consistent."

"And that doesn't drive you crazy? Mr. Everything-In-Its-Optimal-Place?" I challenged, trying to regain my footing.

"I'm discovering that optimal doesn't always mean what I thought it did."

The weight of his gaze, the implication in his words, sent heat spreading through me. I turned back to the bookshelf, my fingers finally closing around the worn, faded blue cloth spine I'd been seeking.

"Here it is." I pulled out the book, its age evident in the softened corners. "First edition of *Patterns in the Visible World* by Eleanor Mitchell. She was a poet fascinated by mathematical concepts and how the same underlying structures appear in both art and science."

Zach approached, his focus shifting to the volume as I placed it carefully in his hands. He opened it to the title page, tracing the author's faded inscription.

"This is remarkable," he said softly. He turned a page with a delicate touch. "Where did you find it?"

"Hidden in the theology section of a dusty used

bookstore in Chicago years ago. The owner didn't know what he had." I moved closer, leaning in to point to a particular passage. My shoulder brushed his arm. Neither of us pulled away. I was hyperaware of our proximity. "This part made me think of you—where she describes algorithms as 'poetry written in the language of mathematics.'"

He looked up from the page, his face inches from mine. "You found this before you met me." His voice was soft and rough.

"Yes."

"And it made you think of me."

"Today it did."

"Theo." My name sounded different on his lips, stripped of professional context, intensely personal. "This arrangement between us..."

"Doesn't feel like an arrangement anymore," I finished for him. The words were risky and true.

Something shifted in his eyes then—a conscious lowering of defenses. I couldn't have said who initiated it. The narrow distance between us vanished. My hand found the back of his neck, fingers tangling in the soft hair at his nape, as our lips met.

It was hesitant at first—a question asked, an answer offered.

Then, a deepening certainty.

He tasted of wine. His hands came to rest at my

waist, the touch tentative for only a beat before pulling me closer.

The book was carefully set aside on a nearby stack of papers as the contact deepened. When we finally broke apart, gasping slightly, his glasses were askew. The sight of always-composed Zach Mendez disheveled by a spontaneous kiss sent a thrill through me.

"That wasn't in the contract." His voice was husky, breathing uneven.

"Definitely unauthorized." The words came out unsteadily. I reached up, adjusting the skewed lenses with trembling fingers, letting them linger against the warmth of his skin for a moment longer than necessary. "We should probably discuss the terms violation."

His hands still rested firmly at my waist, thumbs tracing small, distracting circles against my sides. "From a research perspective, it introduces significant variables."

"Completely compromises objectivity." My gaze dropped to his lips. It was hard to focus on anything else.

"The data will be hopelessly contaminated."

"Terrible scientific practice." I leaned closer still, the pull between us undeniable.

This time, there was no hesitation. The kiss was

immediate, hungry, a release of tension that had been building since our first meeting. My back was against a bookshelf as Zach pressed in. A biography of Ada Lovelace, ironically, tumbled to the floor.

His hands untucked my shirt and slid beneath, cool against my heated skin. He traced my spine with a focused precision that was uniquely, distractingly him

"Wait," he murmured against my mouth. He pulled away just enough to create space for words, though not for breath. His eyes were dark, intense. "We should establish parameters."

I laughed, breathless. "Are you trying to algorithm our kiss?"

His expression was earnest despite his tousled hair and the flush rising on his neck. "I want to make sure there's informed consent in a situation that deviates from our established professional arrangement."

"I'm fully informed," I assured him. My hands rested flat against his chest, feeling the rapid, heavy beat of his heart beneath my palms. "And if you couldn't tell, I'm very much consenting."

"The publicity aspect—" he began.

"Isn't why I'm kissing you." I met his gaze, needing him to understand this fundamental point. "Is it why you're kissing me?"

"No." The denial was swift, absolute. "This has

nothing to do with LoveLogic or your book or any external metrics."

Relief washed through me. "Then we're on the same page." I traced the line of his jaw. "Though I have one parameter to suggest."

"Which is?" he asked. His gaze fixed on my mouth once more.

"Less talking, more kissing."

His smile unfolded slowly, like something he hadn't let himself feel in a long time. Years of careful control seemed to fall away, revealing the unguarded man beneath. "A compelling argument," he conceded.

Then his lips found mine again—fierce and demanding.

A startling thought surfaced. No algorithm, no matter how sophisticated, could have predicted this. The specific, chaotic, undeniable chemistry between us. No data point could capture the feeling of his mouth on me, the heat of his hands on my skin, the way he said my name like it meant something.

A carefully constructed worldview didn't just shift—it collapsed into an exhilaratingly real new reality.

## 14

Zach

"Zach, these metrics are unprecedented." Trina's voice was crisp as she was in full CMO mode. Charts glowed on the big screen—upward curves, impressive percentages. "Sign-ups are up thirty-two percent over projections, and social media sentiment has shifted dramatically positive."

Marketing leads exchanged satisfied glances. Product and development managers nodded. I took a sip of my coffee. The taste registered as merely functional fuel as I absorbed the data, not ready to comment on it.

"The compatibility experiment is driving most of this growth." She swiped to a slide crowded with social media snippets. #LogicWins. #TeamLogic.

Photos of Theo and me. The bookstore entrance, with our heads bent close in conversation. The museum, as we leaned toward each other mid-debate.

My grip tightened on the ceramic mug. The whole thing was reductive. Exploitative. Our interactions, the challenging debates, the unexpected moments of alignment—reduced to marketing assets and social media fodder.

"The narrative has transformed," Trina continued. "What started as a philosophical disagreement has evolved into a compelling relationship story. People are emotionally invested now."

Relationship story. The phrase grated. Was that what this was? A narrative to be consumed?

I couldn't help but think of Marco—charm masking calculation, intimacy weaponized. Different circumstances, yet the feeling of personal connection being leveraged was uncomfortably familiar.

"The next official date isn't scheduled until next week." Trina consulted her tablet. "The formal dinner at Veritas. But this ongoing organic interaction is more valuable from an engagement perspective."

Organic interaction. Clinical. Detached. As if our connection could be plotted on the same graphs as user acquisition rates.

"Let's keep the focus on the technology." My voice was harsher than intended. "The compatibility experiment is a demonstration of LoveLogic's effectiveness, not a reality show."

Trina gave me a curious look, a brief question in her eyes, but nodded. She transitioned smoothly to the next agenda items.

I forced my attention on the topics, nodding at appropriate intervals, contributing analysis when required. Meanwhile, a part of me considered how the clean lines of data blurred against the unquantifiable reality of my feelings for Theo.

"The board is pleased with the publicity metrics." Daniel Park settled into the chair opposite my desk. His presence always seemed like a strategic maneuver, calculated for maximum impact. "Your little experiment is yielding big results."

I resisted the urge to check my phone to see if Theo had sent any texts. "The transparency initiative is driving most of the engagement. Users appreciate understanding the technology behind their matches."

Daniel's thin smile was devoid of warmth. He knew I was deflecting. "Users appreciate the narrative, Zach. The logic versus love dynamic. The apparent evolution from intellectual adversaries to..." He paused, letting the implication hang. "Whatever you two are becoming."

There it was again—our connection framed as a commodity. An icy knot tightened in my stomach.

"Everything about this experiment is relevant to our valuation," Daniel continued. "Your relationship with Barrett has become an unexpected asset."

"It's not an asset. It's not a marketing strategy or a valuation driver. It's—" I caught myself, pulling back from the precipice of revealing something I was still struggling to define to myself.

Daniel's eyebrows arched. "It's what, exactly?"

"It's a more complex interaction than antici-pated. The data is valuable for algorithm refinement."

"I see." Daniel stood, smoothing his immaculate suit jacket. "Well, whatever it is, keep it up. The investors love it, the users love it, and our projected valuation increased by twelve percent."

He left and I turned to the window, staring unseeing at the city skyline.

Twelve percent. The quantified value of my connection with Theo.

The absurdity—and the creeping sense of wrong-ness—was overwhelming. I'd built a company based on quantifying compatibility, and now the commercial success of that company threatened to corrupt the most genuine connection I'd experienced since before LoveLogic existed.

Was this what Theo had been trying to warn me about all along?

---

By EVENING, my internal conflict had solidified into a decision.

The publicity arrangement and whatever was real between Theo and me needed distinct boundaries. I would talk to him at dinner. Establish parameters to separate the personal from the professional.

At 7:30, as I prepared to leave the office, my phone emitted the urgent, discordant chime of a critical system alert. I checked the message: *Pattern recognition module. Anomalous behavior detected.*

My professional instincts snapped into action. Diagnostics first. Dinner could wait. I called Theo, intending to leave a brief voicemail.

"Hey." His voice was immediate and warm.

"I need to postpone dinner." I was already pulling up system dashboards on my main screen. The familiar cascade of data gave me comfort even though there was a problem to deal with. "There's a critical issue with the pattern recognition module that requires troubleshooting."

"The algorithm emergency trumps dinner." Amusement was clear in his tone. "Of course, that's very on-brand."

"I'm sorry." Regret cut through the adrenaline of the crisis. "Rain check?"

"How long do you think you'll be working?"

I scanned the error logs, the complexity of the situation becoming apparent. "Several hours at minimum. This is a core system component."

"Want company?"

The offer was so unexpected it short-circuited my analytical process. "You want to watch me debug code?"

"I want to see how the sausage is made. Research for my book. Plus, I already ordered takeout that can easily be redirected to your office."

A guest. Here. Amidst a potential system crisis.

My usual protocols screamed against it—security, confidentiality, the need for absolute focus.

Yet the thought of Theo's presence, his steadying counterpoint to the digital chaos, was unexpectedly appealing.

"That would be acceptable." The words came

out stiff, not at all what I meant. "I'd like that," I quickly added.

Not long after our call, Thai curry subtly perfumed my office in the dev center. Theo sat across from my desk, discarded takeout containers between us. He watched my screen with an intensity that suggested actual interest rather than polite endurance.

His presence wasn't distracting. It was grounding. I felt relaxed, yet focused on the work.

"So, this pattern you're fixing?" He gestured toward a complex code block with a chopstick. "It's what helps the algorithm identify compatibility factors?"

"It's one component." My fingers moved across the keyboard, diagnosing the error pathway. "This module analyzes communication pattern complementarity. Specifically, how different communication styles might balance each other rather than create friction."

"Like your precision balancing my intuitive approach," Theo observed. The connection was immediate, effortless.

I looked up, meeting his eyes across the scattered remnants of our impromptu dinner. "Exactly like that."

The crisis momentarily faded. In its place was a quiet recognition of what had grown between us.

"What happens when the experiment ends?" Theo asked suddenly. His voice was softer now. "Four dates. That was the agreement. We've done three, with the final dinner just a few days away."

The question landed squarely on the uncertainty I'd been avoiding. We both knew this arrangement had an expiration date. Our connection didn't feel like it did. At least, that's what I hoped.

"I don't know. The parameters have evolved beyond the original scope."

Theo's smile was wide. "That's a very technical way of saying we've completely departed from the script."

"The script was flawed from the beginning." I realized the truth of it as I spoke. "It assumed predictable interaction patterns in an inherently unpredictable domain."

"Human connection."

"Yes." I stopped typing and turned in my chair to face him. The code could wait. This couldn't. "Theo, what happened last night—"

"Was not in the contract." His gaze was steady. "Neither is this conversation. Neither is the fact that I've thought about kissing you again approximately fifty-seven times today."

"You counted?"

"No, but I figured you'd appreciate a quantifiable metric." He gently teased. "Measurable data points matter to you."

He wasn't just teasing—there was something beneath it. The balance, the understanding. It caught me off guard and mattered more than I wanted to admit.

"I need to tell you something." I shouldn't have said it—not here, not now—but I couldn't ignore the need for honesty. "The publicity aspect of this arrangement is generating significant commercial benefit. User engagement is up, investor confidence is strengthening, IPO valuation is increasing."

"That was the point, wasn't it?" Theo's expression grew more serious.

"Yes, but..." I removed my glasses, setting them on the desk. "What's happening between us has nothing to do with that. Nothing to do with the arrangement or the company."

"I know." His voice was quiet, certain.

"Do you?" I asked, needing the reassurance. "Because your critique of algorithmic matching has always centered on the commercialization of human connection. And now our connection is being monetized in real-time metrics."

Theo considered for a moment before answering.

"That's a fair point. But there's a difference between the system and the people in it." He leaned forward, his gaze direct. "I'm not kissing LoveLogic's CEO as part of a publicity stunt. I'm kissing Zach Mendez because I want to."

His certainty cut through my internal conflict, offering a clarity I hadn't been able to find on my own. "Even though our initial connection was brought about by the very algorithm you've criticized?"

"Maybe especially because of that." He stood and moved around the desk, closing the distance between us. "The algorithm created an opportunity —one I would have dismissed without the contract forcing me to spend time with you. But what's developed since then? That's just us."

He stopped beside my chair. I looked up at him, the personal connection overriding everything else.

"The data would suggest we're validating the algorithm's prediction." The scientist in me needed to frame it, even now. "Ninety-two percent compatibility manifesting in actual connection."

Theo reached down, his hand gently cupping my face. The simple touch short-circuited my thoughts, all logic drowned out by the intensity of the sensation. "Or two people connected despite their differences. Not because an algorithm predicted it, but because they chose it."

"Those interpretations aren't mutually exclusive." My voice was uneven.

"No," he agreed as he leaned in. "They're not."

This time, when our lips met, there was no lingering analysis, no calculation of risk versus reward. There was only the undeniable pull toward him. My hands found his waist, pulling him closer, the solid warmth of him an anchor in the swirling complexities of the past few days.

When we finally drew apart, breathless, I was surprised to find myself smiling—not with the managed expression I wore in meetings, but something more unguarded. The smile I had whenever he was around.

Theo's hand was still resting against my face, his thumb tracing the line of my jaw. "For a man who built an algorithm to optimize relationship formation, you're remarkably good at this unscripted human connection thing. I think I'm officially a terrible influence on you, Mendez."

"Adaptation comes naturally when presented with new information." I stood to face him, bringing us eye to eye. "And you, Theo Barrett, are definitely new information."

The urgent chime of the system alert on my

primary monitor brought me back why we were here. The algorithm problem remained unresolved. I glanced at the screen, then back at Theo.

"Algorithmic duty calls," he said, his voice mixed with amusement and resignation.

I reached out and switched the monitor off.

"It can wait."

His eyebrows shot up in genuine surprise. "Zach Mendez, prioritizing kissing over code? The apocalypse must be near."

"Not the end of the world." I drew him closer. "Just an unexpected but statistically significant outlier in my behavioral pattern."

"Stop talking about statistics," Theo murmured, his lips against mine.

For once, ignoring the data was the most logical choice I could make.

# 15

Theo

Nervous butterflies battled it out in my stomach as I walked toward Vivian's office. This meeting wouldn't be easy. The changes I'd made to the manuscript—softening my critique, acknowledging complexity—wouldn't be what she or the publisher expected.

Just get through it, I told myself, pausing outside her door. Defend the truth as you see it.

"Come in," Vivian called as I knocked, her voice sharp.

She sat behind her large desk, a printout of the manuscript spread before her, red marks standing out like fresh wounds against the white paper.

"This isn't what we agreed on, Theo." Vivian slapped the draft on the desk between us. Outside her window, heavy clouds gathering over the city skyline.

"I'm still critical of algorithmic dating." I dropped into the ergonomic chair opposite her, forcing my voice to remain steady. "Now I've got a more nuanced perspective."

"Nuanced?" She leaned forward, her sharp gaze pinning me. One perfectly manicured finger tapped an offending paragraph. "You literally wrote that LoveLogic's approach to transparency 'represents a meaningful step toward ethical algorithmic design.' That's not nuanced—that's endorsement."

Heat prickled my neck. I shifted, resisting the urge to look away.

"It's acknowledgment of improvement." I pictured Zach in his office, explaining the visualization tools with genuine passion. "Their new interface addresses one of my core criticisms about black-box algorithms. Ignoring that wouldn't be intellectually honest."

Vivian studied me, her editorial instincts zeroing in on the actual issue. "This isn't just about their tools and algorithms, is it?"

How could I explain? How could I articulate

that the man whose arguments I'd spent months dismantling was the same one whose touch lingered? Whose vulnerability I'd witnessed? That the very system I'd set out to expose had, impossibly, facilitated a very real connection?

"My research has revealed complexities I didn't initially account for."

"Your research." Her tone dripped skepticism, making the word sound like a flimsy cover story. "You mean your increasingly non-professional interactions with Zach Mendez?"

Before I could formulate a defense, she slid her tablet across the desk. My own face stared back at me, alongside Zach's. A candid shot, blurry but unmistakable, taken outside my apartment building the night of the reading. We weren't touching, not exactly, but the angle, the proximity, the way we leaned slightly towards each other—it radiated an intimacy that couldn't be denied.

My stomach plummeted. The breach was personal, invasive—like someone had reached inside my life without permission. Professional dread crashed in, compounding the violation. "I wasn't aware we were photographed."

"Clearly." Vivian's expression softened, just a fraction. "Look, Theo, I get it. Mendez is charismatic, brilliant, apparently not the soulless technocrat you painted him as. But you signed a contract to write a book critically examining current dating platforms and their impact on authentic human connection."

"Which I'm still doing." I gripped the arms of the chair. "Just with a more complete understanding of the intentions behind these systems. Intentions matter."

"The publisher didn't pay an advance for a philosophical treatise on intentions. They paid for your distinctive critical voice—the perspective that made your initial articles go viral." She tapped the manuscript again, her focus absolute. "This reads like you're hedging your bets. Like you're afraid to land the punch."

The accusation stung because it resonated. Was I pulling back to protect Zach, to protect whatever fragile thing was growing between us?

I weighed the potential professional fallout—the book deal, my reputation as an incisive critic. Then I thought of Zach at the diner, sharing the story of Marco's betrayal. The conflict churned inside me, hot and nauseating.

"What are you asking me to do, Vivian?" My tone was tighter now. "Ignore insights that contradict my original thesis? Twist the narrative to fit a preconceived angle? That's not journalism—it's propaganda."

"I'm asking you to remember why you started this project." Her voice was steady, professional, but her eyes held a warning. "Your father left your mother because an app told him to. These systems have real consequences for real people. Your critique matters. Don't lose sight of that because you've developed feelings for one developer."

The raw mention of my parents felt like turning a knife. How could I explain that watching Zach, seeing his genuine struggle with the ethics of his own creation, had made me question the very nature of blame? That maybe the algorithm wasn't the villain, but a mirror reflecting human desires and flaws?

"I can still be critical while acknowledging complexity." The words were a declaration I wasn't sure I could hold. "A one-dimensional takedown doesn't serve readers any better than a laudatory puff piece."

Vivian sighed, leaning back in her chair, her tension easing. "The publisher won't be happy with complexity. They want clarity. Conflict."

"Then they can reject the manuscript." The conviction behind my words surprised me. "I won't write something I don't believe anymore just to fulfill a contract."

"And what do you believe now, Theo?"

It was a question I'd been wrestling. I took a slow breath, finding my footing in the shifting landscape of my beliefs.

"I believe these systems have significant limitations and ethical concerns that need constant scrutiny. But I also believe they can reflect genuine attempts to solve real human problems of loneliness and connection. The intentions behind them, the choices people make using them—those matter alongside the outcomes."

"Intentions don't generate book sales," Vivian pointed out, ever the pragmatist. "Controversy does."

"Then I need to find a way to make nuance controversial," I muttered, my fighting spirit returning.

A reluctant smile touched her lips. "Now that would be a publishing miracle." She gathered the manuscript pages, straightening them. "Rewrite the introduction and conclusion. Keep your new insights but sharpen your critique. Find the tension in the complexity. Give me something I can defend to the publisher."

It wasn't a complete victory, but it was a path forward, a way to potentially reconcile my evolving perspective with my professional obligations. "I'll try."

"Do better than try." She stuffed the manuscript into a folder and put it aside. "And Theo?" Her voice held a different note as I stood to leave. "Whatever's happening between you and Mendez... just be careful. Personal involvement always complicates professional judgment."

Vivian, sharp as ever, saw the tightrope I was walking.

"One more thing," she called out, before I got to the door. "The publisher's reviewing photos for the book jacket—they're thinking of using one of you and Mendez from the museum debate. That confrontational energy sells."

The irony was almost physical. "I'll keep that in mind."

Outside, rain had started, fat drops splattering against the sidewalk. I tugged my collar higher and considered the weight of the choices ahead. My phone buzzed in my pocket. I pulled it to check the notification.

Mom: *Invite your algorithm man to dinner tonight. I want to meet him properly.*

I stopped dead on the sidewalk, rain plastering my hair to my forehead, and read the message again. My mother had invited Zach—*my algorithm man*—to dinner. The woman whose life had been upended by algorithmic certainty wanted to break bread with the architect of a similar system?

I called her immediately, ducking under the inadequate shelter of a bus stop awning.

"Mom? Did you just... invite Zach Mendez to dinner?"

"Hello to you too, Theodore." Her voice, warm and familiar, carried its usual blend of academic accuracy and paternal affection. "And yes, I did. Is that a problem?"

"It's unexpected." I wiped rain from my face. "After everything, your feelings about online dating have been pretty clear."

"I've been clear about my feelings toward people who abandon thirty-year marriages because an app told them to," she corrected gently. "That doesn't mean I can't be civilized toward your... whatever he is."

Her slight hesitation before that last phrase wasn't lost on me. "He's a subject I'm writing about," I said, even though he was more than that.

"Mmm." That sound conveyed a universe of maternal skepticism. "Your manuscript suggests something more complex than subject and journalist. Vivian sends your drafts to me, you know."

Of course she did.

Annoyance warred with vulnerability. My mother was witnessing my professional and personal turmoil unfold in draft form. "Everyone seems very invested in maintaining my critical stance." I couldn't keep the edge from my voice.

"I'm more interested in understanding why it's shifting." She stayed calm. "Hence, dinner. Seven o'clock. Bring wine. Something robust, I think."

She hung up before I could argue, protest, or understand the implications.

My mother wanted to meet Zach. In her home. The home haunted by the ghost of algorithmic disruption. The potential for disaster was enormous. Yet, beneath my anxiety, there was also hope.

I stayed under the awning, rain drumming a steady rhythm around me, and texted Zach, trying to inject a casualness I didn't feel.

Theo: *Unexpected development: my mother would like you to join us for dinner tonight. You can decline if it's too weird/personal/potentially requires hazard pay.*

His response came almost immediately.

Zach: *I'd be honored. Should I bring anything?*

The simple, unhesitating acceptance sent a wave of warmth through me, amplifying my hope. This was happening. Zach was entering my personal history, which was the very heart of my critique.

Theo: *Just your best algorithmic defense. She's a formidable opponent. Don't let the PhD in psychology fool you.*

Zach: *So I've gathered from your writings. Perhaps I should run simulations of potential conversation patterns beforehand.*

I laughed, startling a woman huddled beside me under the awning. Was he joking? With Zach, it was sometimes hard to tell.

Theo: *Just be yourself. The real you, not the CEO version. The one who talks about his abuela.*

Three dots appeared, vanished, reappeared. His response, when it came, showed how the thought he'd put into it.

Zach: *They're not entirely separate entities, but I understand your meaning. I'll aim for authenticity over optimization.*

The phrasing was so distinctly Zach—that blend of analytical framing and genuine intention. I smiled again despite the drumming rain and the weight of the choices ahead. This crossing of worlds, this collision course between my professional life, my personal history, and the man who embodied the intersection of both. It was terrifying. And necessary.

As I started to walk again, my phone buzzed with another message.

Zach: *For what it's worth, I'm looking forward to*

*understanding more of what shaped you. Context matters in pattern analysis.*

It was so uniquely him. It crystallized everything. Yes, the risks were real for how this could impact me. But the connection between us wasn't something to avoid. It needed to be explored. And the reward? It could be significant.

"You're hovering." My mother watched me rearrange the serving dishes on the dining table for the third time. The scent of roasting chicken and herbs filled the small house, a steady comfort beneath my tightly wound nerves.

"It's not hovering." I nudged the breadbasket a millimeter to the left. "I'm ensuring optimal placement for efficient self-service."

"Mmm." That skeptical sound again.

She leaned against the kitchen doorway, in the deep blue dress I recognized from academic conferences. Her analytical gaze missed nothing. "You've also refolded the napkins twice and checked your phone countless times in the past hour. One might develop hypotheses about such anxious pre-guest behavior."

"Or one might just slice the bread instead of

psychoanalyzing her stressed out son," I countered, though the edge was all pretend.

She smiled, pushing off the doorframe and coming to stand beside me at the sideboard. "You're nervous." She tilted her head, just slightly. "That's interesting. Why?"

"It's not nerves." I paused, searching for a more accurate, less revealing word. "I'm concerned about potential conversational land mines detonating over dinner."

"Such as whether online dating contributed to the way my marriage fell apart?" Her directness, honed by decades in academia, still had the power to take my breath away. "I'm not planning to ambush your young man with my personal grievances, Theo. Relax."

"He's not my young man," I mumbled. Relief washed over me at her reassurance. "And thank you. I appreciate that."

She squeezed my arm gently. "I'm curious, Theo, not combative. I've read his recent interviews, the ones about the algorithm anomaly. His perspective on transparency is more nuanced than I credited him with."

My head snapped up. "You've been researching him?"

"Of course." She moved back toward the kitchen.

"I apply the same intellectual rigor to understanding my son's significant... associations... as I do to my academic subjects."

Before I could protest the word *associations*, the doorbell rang. My pulse gave an embarrassing leap. Taking a steadying breath, I went to answer it.

Zach stood on the porch, illuminated by the golden light spilling from the entryway. He was dressed casually in black jeans and a maroon cashmere sweater. In his hands were a bottle of wine and an elegant gift bag. A hint of nervousness flickered behind his composed expression.

"I don't think you could've been more precisely on time." I stepped back.

"Punctuality is important in a first impression." His smile was small but and did ridiculous things to my insides. "Though I confess I drove around the block once to avoid arriving early."

The admission, that glimpse of his internal conflict between ingrained habit and social awareness, was endearing. I wanted to reach out, smooth the barely-there crease between his brows.

And I wanted to kiss him.

Instead, I took his coat. Our fingers brushed, sending an electric jolt through me. "My mother's curious to meet you." I led him toward the kitchen.

"Huh. That's a significant downgrade from the

*formidable opponent* warning you issued in your text." His voice was low and amused.

We entered just as Mom was turning from the oven, holding a steaming platter. She set it down carefully and turned, her sharp gaze sweeping over Zach in a swift, comprehensive assessment.

"Dr. Barrett." Zach stepped forward, hand extended. The nervousness I'd glimpsed moments before was gone, replaced by a quiet confidence. "Thank you for inviting me. I've read several of your papers on attachment theory and technological mediation in relationships. Your work on digital intimacy barriers was foundational to some of LoveLogic's early communication pattern analysis."

I blinked. He hadn't just researched her. He'd read her work. Even incorporated it into his. Seriously?

A flicker of surprise crossed her features as she shook his hand. "That's not something I expected to hear, Mr. Mendez. Most technologists dismiss social psychology as too soft for their predictive models."

"Computational models without psychological frameworks are just math. They might identify correlations but miss the causative mechanisms that drive human interaction." He offered her the gift bag. "I brought wine, but also this. It reminded me of your work on mediated emotional expression."

Mom pulled out a small cloth-bound book. Letters between Marie and Pierre Curie. Her features, usually so controlled, softened as she turned it over in her hands, tracing the embossed title.

"Scientific minds expressing deeply human connection through the technology of their time—written correspondence," Zach explained. "The medium changes across generations, but the fundamental human desire for connection remains constant. I think your work highlights that beautifully."

The thoughtfulness, the specific relevance of the gift—it disarmed her. I saw the walls of her skepticism crumble, replaced by intellectual curiosity and, perhaps, a grudging respect.

"That's quite perceptive, Mr. Mendez." Her voice lacked its usual critical edge.

"Please, call me Zach." He smiled warmly.

As dinner unfolded, Mom, true to form, dove straight into the ethical deep end—algorithmic bias, data privacy, the erosion of personal agency.

To my surprise, Zach didn't flinch. He responded with thoughtfulness, even citing some of her own work, and outlined a more human-centered vision for LoveLogic than I'd ever heard in public statements. Over dessert, he said, "A 98% compatibility score isn't a guarantee—it's a starting point. The rest still depends on human complexity."

Mom raised an eyebrow. "Yet your marketing frames it as certainty."

"Based on some of my conversation with Theo, we're starting to shift that toward choice, not prediction."

I found myself more observer than participant, amazed by their shared intellectual fluency. There was no posturing—just mutual respect. Zach wasn't performing. He was listening, learning, engaging.

"The most meaningful technology," Zach continued, "doesn't replace human judgment—it creates better conditions for it to thrive."

Mom's gaze slid to me, subtle but sharp. "That's not exactly the perspective Theo conveyed in his articles."

Zach didn't hesitate. "My public statements haven't always reflected the nuance of my views. And maybe Theo's interpretation was shaped by his own skepticism."

"Or perhaps you've both evolved in your thinking through this process." Mom's perceptiveness sliced through the polite discourse.

Later, clearing the table while Mom made coffee, the domesticity of working side-by-side with Zach was surprisingly natural. Our movements fell into an easy rhythm.

"She's exactly as formidable as you described." He stacked plates with characteristic precision.

"And yet you seem to have charmed her with nineteenth-century scientific correspondence." I couldn't resist a smile. "Impressive strategy."

"Not calculated, if that's what you're thinking." He met my eyes, his expression open, vulnerable in a way that caught me off guard. "I genuinely thought she'd appreciate them. Her work resonates with their journey."

The sincerity of his words made my chest ache. I wanted to kiss him right there amid the dinner dishes. Instead, I bumped his shoulder lightly with mine, a small acknowledgment that I hoped he interpreted as I meant it.

As Zach prepared to leave, Mom handed him a copy of her book on technological mediation. "My perspective may challenge some of your assumptions, but dialogue across different viewpoints matters. That's something few people understand these days."

"Including me, until recently." He accepted the book with appreciation. His eyes met mine, another silent acknowledgment passing between us.

At the door, Mom stunned me. She reached up

and kissed Zach's cheek. "Take care with my son's heart," she said, just loud enough for me to overhear. "It's more fragile than his argumentative nature might suggest."

"Mom!"

She ignored me. "Goodnight, Zach. You're welcome back anytime."

I joined Zach on the porch and, after she'd closed the door, we stood there, the cool night air a sudden contrast to the warmth inside.

"I like her."

"She likes you too." I was still trying to process the evening's trajectory. "Which is statistically improbable and more than a little scary."

"Afraid we'll compare notes on your delightful contradictions?"

"Mortified," I admitted, only half-joking. We stood in silence for a moment, the importance of the evening settling between us. My mother's acceptance wasn't just personal—it bridged the gap between professional critique and personal truth.

"Theo, I know this complicates your book. Meeting your mother, seeing a different side..."

"Yes." The single word encompassed a universe of complexity.

"What will you do?" His eyes searched mine.

It was the question Vivian had asked. The question I'd been wrestling since the museum visit.

But after this evening, the answer had crystalized. "Write something true. Even if it's more complicated than what the publisher signed up for. Even if it means acknowledging that the lines aren't as clear as I once thought."

He nodded, understanding the professional risk. "For what it's worth, I respect your integrity—even when it's aimed critically at my work."

"And I respect that you faced my mother's skepticism with honesty rather than defensiveness. That means more than you know."

I stepped closer, drawn by an impulse that was both familiar and newly uncomplicated. We kissed briefly under the dim porch light.

"I should go," Zach said, though neither of us moved.

"You should."

His hand found mine, fingers lacing through mine with easy confidence. "Have you thought about what happens after the final arranged date?"

"We should talk about that." The prospect didn't seem like a problem to solve, but more of a conversation to have.

"But not tonight. This was..." He hesitated,

searching for the right word. "Significant. In ways I'm still processing."

I smiled, recognizing his need to analyze the evening.

"Give me time." He returned my smile. "This is a complex new algorithm."

"Of course."

After he left, I went back inside and found Mom in the living room, ostensibly reading but clearly waiting.

"Well?" I asked, sinking onto the couch beside her.

"He's not what I expected. There's depth beneath the technological certainty—a genuine desire to help people, even if his methods differ from mine."

"That doesn't sound like a ringing endorsement."

"It's not an indictment either." She studied me for a moment. "The question isn't what I think of him. It's how knowing him is shifting your thinking."

I hesitated. "It is shifting. I'm seeing more of the human intent behind the tech. It doesn't excuse everything, but... there's more involved with this than I realized."

She nodded. "That kind of tension makes for better thinking. And better writing. Let your book reflect that."

Her words echoed Vivian's earlier. And just like that, the need to justify my perspective eased—replaced by permission to let it evolve.

---

LATER THAT NIGHT, back in my apartment, I opened my laptop. The blinking cursor was no longer mocking. It was inviting.

Words flowed, different from what I'd planned. I wrote about algorithms and authenticity, about intention and impact, about the human heart behind the code. I wrote about Zach, not as a symbol but as a person, complex and contradictory, challenging my assumptions in ways that had ultimately strengthened my understanding.

A text pinged.

Zach: *Your mother asked questions I'll be considering for days. Intellectual rigor clearly runs in the family. Thank you for sharing that part of your world with me.*

A warmth, uncomplicated and sure, spread through me.

Theo: *She's already requested that you join us for Sunday dinner next week. Consider yourself inducted into the Barrett academic debate society. Fair warning: She assigns readings.*

His reply came quickly.

Zach: *I accept with appropriate scholarly humility. Though next time I'll bring more research notes. And perhaps a statistical analysis of Curie's correspondence patterns.*

I laughed, leaning back in my chair, my manuscript on the screen.

The story was shifting, evolving into something richer. More true. Like the connection that had sparked it.

16

Zach

THE LOW HUM of the computers in the dev center were usually comforting, the sound of controlled logic processing predictable data. Tonight, it had become a countdown timer ticking away.

It was nearly midnight. Pre-IPO reports lay ignored on one corner of my desk, reminders of the external pressures rendered insignificant compared to the tangle of code shimmering on my primary monitor.

Riley had run an analysis on the pattern recognition model as a postmortem to the concerning behavior it showed a few days ago. He'd reported several potential areas that needed urgent review.

The team and I had spent hours submerged in

the complex architecture. Any issues had to be found and fix as quick as possible.

My fingers flew across the keyboard, initiating another simulation run. Variation nine. Parameters adjusted to isolate the weighting function for complementary communication styles. Each nanosecond stretched, thick with a dread that had nothing to do with market confidence or board approval.

This was about Theo.

I stood, needing to move. My hand went to my glasses, adjusting them for the fourth time in ten minutes—an unnecessary gesture. A physical manifestation of the internal system error I was experiencing.

Six months ago, this anomaly would have registered as a technical challenge, a problem to be solved with logic. Now it weighed on me—a potential invalidation of something I hadn't even realized I valued.

The simulation completed. Results flashed across the screen. I leaned closer, forcing my focus through the fog of personal anxiety. The numbers stared back, clinical and unforgiving. Riley had indeed found an issue. Under the specific parameters matching Theo's cognitive framework and mine—the module amplified the weighting for complementary traits.

Significantly.

Twelve to fifteen percent inflation. Our 92% compatibility score, the one that read like both cosmic joke and undeniable pull, likely hovered somewhere in the high seventies.

Still significant. Statistically strong. But not the near-certainty the initial number implied. Not the validation I'd been clinging to.

I sank back into my chair, the ergonomic support offering no relief. The professional implications were immediate and severe—disclosure obligations, investor panic, potential IPO derailment.

But the personal fallout landed with seismic force. How could I tell Theo? The man whose entire critique centered on algorithmic manipulation, whose deepest wounds came from technology distorting human connection?

My phone buzzed. Trina chased an update on the disclosure strategy I was supposed to be finalizing. I ignored it, silencing the device.

Compartmentalization. That had always been the key. Keep the personal separate from the professional. The emotional shielded by the logical. But Theo had breached those firewalls, deliberately and irrevocably.

A soft knock sounded at my door. My head snapped up, expecting Riley with more data or Trina refusing to be ignored. Instead, Theo stood there, holding a brown paper bag that radiated the unmistakable scent of vindaloo.

He waited in the doorway like some cosmic twist of fate—proof the universe had a sense of timing I didn't appreciate. Warmth—the automatic pleasure that his presence sparked—was instantly extinguished by a wave of panic.

He couldn't see this. Not yet. Not under these conditions.

"Your security guard called me." Theo stepped inside with that calm confidence that disrupted my equilibrium. His arrival was a vibrant, undeniably sexy variable. "Apparently you've been here for fourteen hours straight and haven't eaten since breakfast."

"Edward called you?" My voice came out tight, stressed. I forced myself into professional mode, though the cracks were already showing.

"We've become friendly during my research visits." Theo's gaze swept over my desk, then sharpened as it landed on the primary monitor, still displaying the diagnostic results. He set the food bag down, his focus narrowing with the instinct I knew so well. "Though he made me promise not to publish that LoveLogic's workaholic CEO needs to be reminded to eat."

I reached to minimize the screens, but it was too late.

"That's the compatibility algorithm." Theo stepped closer, his perceptive eyes missing nothing. "Are those our profiles in the test case?"

There was no escaping it. Lying seemed impossible, even counterproductive. But the full truth—its origins, its implications—was dangerous to share without careful calibration.

I stood, needing to create distance as he moved nearer.

"It is. I'm running validation tests on the pattern recognition module."

"At midnight?" He studied my face, not with accusation, but with the penetrating curiosity that made our debates so compelling and his presence now so difficult. "What's wrong, Zach?"

Transparency, the principle I'd championed, warred with self-preservation. Past betrayals had honed the instinct. I took off my glasses.

Honesty was required. But controlled. Limited.

"Riley was following up on the issue from the other night and found potential anomalies." I kept my voice level, filtering any tremor of anxiety. "I'm working with the team on his findings."

Theo set the bag of food aside, his full attention

now on me, his sparring energy replaced by concern. "What kind of anomalies?"

"A weighting bias in the pattern recognition module. Under specific conditions, the algorithm may amplify certain compatibility factors more than intended."

I searched his face for any sign of skepticism, or the triumphant spark of 'I told you so.' Instead, understanding dawned in his expression as he connected the technical detail to its personal implication.

"Our match." It wasn't a question.

I nodded, bracing myself. "The anomaly seems to activate under very specific profile pairings. Ours appears to be one of them."

Theo was silent for a moment, absorbing the information.

He didn't look angry or vindicated, just thoughtful. That analytical mind, the one that mirrored mine in unexpected ways, was processing. "How significant is the discrepancy?"

"That's what I'm determining now." I gestured toward the screens, relieved he wasn't immediately jumping to conclusions. "Initial findings suggest a potential inflation of twelve to fifteen percent in our compatibility score."

"Making us what? High seventies instead of low nineties?" His tone remained unnervingly neutral.

"Approximately, yes."

He moved to the window, looking out at the city lights, his back to me. The silence stretched, filled with unspoken questions. This was it—the moment where the flaw in our algorithmic origin story could shatter everything that had grown since. I held my breath, waiting for the judgment and critique.

"Does it matter?" He turned to face me finally, his expression still unreadable.

"Does what matter?"

"The exact percentage." He gestured toward the screens, while his eyes stayed on me. "Seventy-seven or ninety-two—does the number actually change anything about what's happened between us?"

His perspective—so focused on the lived reality over the originating data—was the opposite of what I'd expected. It momentarily silenced the storm of corporate and personal anxieties swirling within me.

"From a personal standpoint, no. What's developed between us has transcended any algorithm prediction."

"But from a corporate standpoint?" His journalistic instinct zeroed in on the remaining issue.

"From a corporate standpoint, it's potentially significant." The stress settled back onto my shoulders. "We've built marketing claims and user trust around specific compatibility thresholds. If those thresholds contain unidentified biases…"

"It undermines the product's validity." His understanding was immediate. "And it's happening in the middle of your valuation period."

I nodded, even as a sense of relief mingled with the ongoing dread. He understood the stakes, both professional and personal. "I need to verify the exact scope before determining appropriate disclosure and mitigation strategies."

Theo was quiet again. This time, the silence seemed less analytical. "How long have you known about this?"

"Riley identified earlier today. We've been verifying it since."

"And when were you planning to tell me?" The question was soft, but it landed with precision.

Doubt caused me to hesitate. "I hadn't decided. I wanted to understand the full scope first."

"To protect LoveLogic or to protect me?"

"Both," I said honestly. "The corporate implications are clear. The personal implications are… less so."

Theo moved closer again. There was no judgment in his gaze—just concern. "You're worried this undermines what's happening between us. That I'll see it as confirmation that algorithmic matching is fundamentally flawed."

He saw my fear.

"The thought had occurred to me."

To my astonishment, Theo laughed—a soft, low sound that seemed wildly out of place amidst the crisis. "Zach, I've been critiquing algorithmic dating platforms for years. I never expected LoveLogic to be infallible."

"Then what did you expect?"

"I expected to maintain a professional distance and write my critique." He closed the remaining space between us, resting a hand on my arm. The brief contact sent an unexpected and pleasant jolt through my system. "I didn't expect to discover that the man behind the algorithm was worth knowing beyond his professional creation."

His words, his touch, his understanding—it bypassed my defenses, settling deep in my core. "The anomaly doesn't invalidate our complementary patterns the algorithm identified." I needed him to grasp the technical nuance alongside the emotional one. "It just potentially overstated their significance."

"I don't need statistical significance to know what I feel when I'm with you." His hand tightened on my arm, a grounding point in my swirling uncertainty. "The algorithm created an opportunity.

Everything since has been our choice, not computational prediction."

His certainty calmed the storm within me. This wasn't ammunition. Not a validation of his critique at the expense of our connection. He was separating the issues by seeing the human element beyond the technological flaw.

"I still need to resolve this professionally." The path forward felt clearer knowing where he stood. "Users and investors deserve transparency."

"Of course they do. That's the right decision. But Zach—" He waited until I looked at him. "This doesn't change anything between us."

Relief washed through me, potent and clarifying.

"The food's getting cold." He gestured to the bag on my desk with a hint of his usual teasing warmth. "And you need to eat before you make any major corporate decisions."

I managed a smile, the first one I'd had all day. "Very sensible approach."

"One of us has to be practical." He was already unpacking containers. The fragrant scent of curry and naan filled the air.

We ate standing near the window, the city lights reflecting in the glass. Theo asked sharp technical questions and offered perspectives on disclosure strategy. His journalist's mind engaged the problem without judgment.

"What's your next step?" He leaned against the window frame beside me as we finished. "Professionally speaking."

"Complete verification of the anomaly's scope and impact. Then develop disclosure and mitigation strategies for users and investors. Full transparency."

"And personally?"

His focused gaze helped the truth click into place. "I need to separate LoveLogic's technical challenges from what's happening between us. They're related but distinct issues."

"Good answer. Though I'd expect nothing less from someone who can simultaneously debug code and maintain emotional compartmentalization."

"My compartmentalization skills have been significantly compromised recently." The corner of my mouth twitched upward.

He leaned closer, the shared understanding creating an intimacy that was more potent than any physical touch. "For what it's worth, this anomaly you've discovered—I think it actually strengthens your integrity. You're willing to investigate potential flaws in your own system rather than ignore them for commercial convenience."

His perspective shifted my internal narrative again, reframing crisis as character test.

Theo glanced at his watch. "I should go. It's after one, and you need to finish up so you can get some rest."

"You're right, of course." Though the thought of him leaving reignited the earlier anxiety.

As he gathered the empty food containers, I acted on impulse, catching his hand before he could turn away. His skin was warm against mine.

"Thank you." The words were inadequate for what he'd done. "For the food, but more importantly, for the perspective."

"Anytime." His thumb brushed against my knuckles. "Though maybe next time we could meet under less professionally complicated circumstances."

"I'd like that."

The crisis receded, leaving only the pull between us. I leaned in. He met me halfway. Our kiss was a quiet confirmation—shared understanding without words.

When we separated, his eyes searched mine. "We have a bad habit of flaunting the rules of the publicity arrangement contract. Not that I'm complaining."

"I believe we've established multiple precedents for exceeding contractual parameters."

"True." He squeezed my hand once more before releasing it, gathering his coat. "Call me later? After you've rested and made your decisions?"

"I will."

After he left, the hum of the servers returned—comforting, but not nearly as much as his presence. The line between personal and professional had blurred beyond recognition, but the work remained. The anomaly still waited. And so did my responsibility to face it.

My phone buzzed. A message notification on the secured network. Edward, from building security.

Edward: *Sir, regarding your visitor this evening—protocol requires me to remind that all after-hours access is recorded by security cameras. The footage is automatically archived for 30 days.*

I froze, reading the message again.

Recorded. Automatically archived. Our kiss.

The visual evidence of our relationship evolving far beyond professional parameters.

Dread, sharp and distinct from the earlier professional anxiety, washed over me. One crisis averted, only to be replaced by another, far more personal threat. I typed back.

Zach: *Thank you for the reminder, Edward. Standard security protocols are appropriate.*

But as I stared at the phone, I knew nothing about this situation was standard.

# 17

Theo

My coffee mug slipped, clattering against my countertop as a message flashed across my phone screen.

Vivian: *Check Techscape now. Your "research" just went viral.*

I tapped the link. The page loaded, displaying a grainy still image that made my blood run cold.

Security footage. Zach's office. Us.

The timestamp showed a little after 1 AM, two nights ago. We stood close, my hands moving to his waist as he kissed me.

Not a casual kiss. The kind that screamed intimacy, vulnerability, a story neither of us was ready to tell.

"Shit." My heart hammered in my chest. I scrolled down, forcing myself to read the accompanying article.

*ALGORITHM PROVES ITSELF? LoveLogic Founder and Critic Caught in Late-Night Embrace*

Anonymous source. Access to company security. Questions whether the publicity arrangement evolved into genuine connection.

The clinical dissection of something so personal felt...

My phone rang, shrill and demanding. Audrey, my literary agent. Of course.

"Have you seen it?" she demanded when I answered.

"Just now." I stumbled toward my window, peering through the blinds as if paparazzi might materialize on the sidewalk below. "How bad is this?"

"Bad? This is publishing gold!" Her voice crackled, filled with excitement, completely at odds with the sick churning in my gut. "The hook for your book just wrote itself! Dating algorithm critic falls for algorithm creator—we couldn't have scripted better publicity!"

"This isn't publicity, Audrey." Protectiveness surged through me—for Zach, for whatever fragile thing existed between us. "This is a disgusting invasion of privacy."

"A security camera in a corporate office isn't a private bedroom." Audrey's logic sliced through my emotional reaction. "Besides, you're both public figures engaged in a documented compatibility experiment. It was always going to attract attention. The publisher wants an emergency meeting at eleven. Be there."

She hung up. I stared at the article still burning on the screen.

Publishing gold? My stomach roiled.

I tried calling Zach, needing to hear his voice and gauge his reaction. Straight to voicemail. I gripped the phone tighter, typing a text with unsteady thumbs.

Theo: *Have you seen Techscape? We need to talk before I meet with my publisher.*

Three dots appeared, vanished, reappeared. Finally, after what seemed like minutes, the message arrived.

Zach: *In crisis management meetings. Breach traced to night security contractor. Call you when I can.*

Professional. Controlled. The brevity screamed chaos.

While Audrey saw publicity gold, Zach was

dealing with a corporate security incident, a potential disaster weeks before the company's IPO. Our orbits, professional and personal, had just violently collided.

I showered, the hot water doing little to ease the chill inside me. As I dressed my journalist brain, the one I'd been trying to quiet, pushed forward with a question I couldn't ignore: How did security footage from LoveLogic's fortress leak? A night contractor? Possible, but convenient. A breach like this hinted at deeper vulnerabilities. The kind of story I was built to chase.

Except the thought of chasing it, of digging into Zach's crisis for my own gain, made bile rise in my throat.

THE PUBLISHER'S conference room felt like an icebox—all glass and steel and judgment. Vivian sat opposite me, Audrey beside her, flanked by marketing and publicity heads. The leaked video played on a massive screen behind them—us, kissing, over and over.

"We're shifting the entire promotional campaign," Vivian said. "The video changes everything."

I sat rigid, hands clenched in my lap beneath the table, watching my personal life dissected as a branding opportunity.

"The early manuscript pages hint at your evolving perspective," she continued. "But now we can frame it as a journey from skeptic to believer—not just in the algorithm, but in its creator."

"I'm not a *believer* in algorithmic dating." I re-emphasized the points I'd already made to Vivian. "My perspective has become more nuanced, not completely reversed. The critique remains."

"Nuance doesn't sell books." The marketing head echoed the sentiment Vivian had in our previous meeting. "Transformation does. Critic falls for subject is a story readers understand. It's relatable. Human."

"It's not that simple." Heat rose in my neck.

"It absolutely is that simple." The publicity director leaned forward. "The video already has over two million views. #LogicWins is trending. People are fascinated by the notion that the algorithm might have been right all along."

I recoiled internally. #LogicWins. As if our connection was some kind of validation for his system.

"If you actually read my manuscript draft, you'd know that's not my conclusion." My voice carried deliberate sharpness. "The human bond that developed between Zach and me isn't an endorsement of the algorithm. It's evidence that connection goes beyond technological prediction. It emerged despite our differences, not because some code predicted it."

They stared at me, calculation flickering in their eyes.

"That's a less commercial angle." The marketing director's disappointment was palpable.

"But it's the true one." I met his gaze. "And it's the book I'm writing."

The rest of the meeting passed in a blur of strategic rebranding. My phone remained stubbornly silent. No word from Zach. Was he okay? Was he shutting me out? The uncertainty gnawed at me, a physical ache beneath my ribs.

As we wrapped up, Sarah, a junior editor I barely knew, approached hesitantly, her expression sympathetic.

"Sorry about the timing." She glanced around to ensure we weren't overheard.

"Of the leak?" I forced a casual tone. "Not your fault."

"No." She shook her head, lowering her voice further. "Of the algorithm issues."

My blood ran cold again. "What issues?"

"My roommate works at *VentureTech News*.

They're running a piece tomorrow about LoveLogic identifying critical weaknesses in their matching algorithm. Apparently, it affects high-engaging matches..." She trailed off, giving me a pointed look. "Including yours."

My stomach plummeted. Zach's late-night work. The anomaly.

This was the story. Potential algorithmic flaws. The matches affected. Weeks before the IPO. It was journalistic dynamite.

"How reliable is this information?" I asked, my voice sounding distant, detached, like a journalist assessing a lead.

"Reliable enough, from what I've heard, that three separate outlets are chasing it." Sarah looked genuinely apologetic. "I just thought you should know, given your... situation."

She scurried away, leaving me rooted to the spot. The story was perfect. Explosive. The kind of critical validation my publisher craved. All I had to do was pursue it. Confirm the rumors. Connect the dots.

And betray Zach completely.

The thought made me physically ill. I drifted toward the elevators, pulling out my phone. Zach's voicemail answered.

"It's me. I just heard about potential leaks regarding algorithm issues. Call me. Please."

Vivian caught me before the elevator arrived. "We need to talk about the LoveLogic algorithm."

I kept my face blank. "What are you talking about?"

"Don't play dumb, Theo. Half the tech journalism world is chasing rumors about flaws in their matching system." Her eyes narrowed. "Did you know about this?"

The direct question hung in the air between us, heavy with implication. Professional obligation versus personal loyalty. The core of my conflict laid bare.

"What exactly are you asking me, Vivian?"

"I'm asking if you have insider information about LoveLogic's algorithm that you haven't shared with your editor." Her tone was clipped, businesslike, but the accusation resonated. "Details that would be central to the book we're publishing. Things you might have learned personally?"

This was the ethical precipice. Admit knowledge, become the source, betray Zach's trust?

Or deflect, protect him, and compromise my journalistic standing?

"If I had privileged information offered in confidence, I wouldn't discuss it without the source's permission." I choose each word as if I was navigating a minefield.

Vivian's expression hardened. "Sources don't get to dictate coverage, Theo. You know that."

A surprising firmness settled within me. "They do when the details were shared in a personal rather than professional context."

"And which context were you operating in when you kissed the subject of your book in his office at midnight?" Her question landed like a physical blow. Targeted. Accurate. "The lines are blurred, Theo. That's the problem."

She was right. The boundaries weren't just blurred. They'd been obliterated. My ethics were tangled hopelessly with my personal feelings.

"I need to talk to Zach before I discuss this further."

"Your personal relationship is your business. But your professional obligations are non-negotiable. If LoveLogic's algorithm has flaws affecting their public claims, and you have information about it, that's central to your book. Don't forget that."

I stepped into the elevator, desperate for escape. "I'll call you later."

The doors slid shut, leaving me alone with the crushing weight of my conflicting loyalties. I could write the story that would solidify my reputation, validate my initial critique, and satisfy my publisher. All it would cost was Zach's trust and whatever fragile, unexpected bond had grown between us.

Or I could choose differently. Prioritize the human connection over the professional scoop. Risk my career for something less tangible but potentially more meaningful.

The choice seemed impossible. And unavoidable.

By evening, the leaked video dominated tech news, now interwoven with speculative pieces about LoveLogic's algorithm integrity. My phone buzzed relentlessly—colleagues fishing for details. I ignored them all, pacing my apartment like a caged animal.

I drafted and deleted numerous texts to Zach.

How could I bridge the gap without sounding like I was digging for information?

The knock on my door wasn't tentative. Three quick raps. Firm. Urgent.

My heart leaped. I opened it to find Zach standing there, looking utterly wrecked. Hair disheveled, tie loosened, collar unbuttoned. I saw the exhaustion etched around his eyes.

"Can I come in?" His voice was rough, strained.

Relief warred with a sudden, sharp apprehension. "I've been trying to reach you all day."

"I know." He moved past me, his usual deliberate grace replaced by a restless, frayed energy. "My communication has been... restricted by corporate counsel."

"Because of the video or the algorithm issues?" I asked, closing the door, the air crackling with unspoken tension.

He turned, surprise flickering in his tired eyes. "You know about both."

I nodded even though it wasn't a question. "The video was hard to miss. And I heard the rumors about the algorithm flaws from a publishing colleague."

His expression shuttered, a subtle closing off that made my chest ache. "So you've been gathering information for your book."

The suspicion in his voice and the assumption of my motives flared frustration. "No." I snapped, moving closer. "I've been worried sick about you."

"While simultaneously receiving journalistic tips about LoveLogic's technical challenges." His tone remained unnervingly even, but I saw the tremor in his hand as he pushed his glasses up. "Very efficient multitasking."

"That's not fair, Zach! I haven't pursued any of

those leads. I ignored them. I've been waiting to hear from you."

"Waiting to get the story direct from the source?" The bitterness in his voice was stark, unfamiliar.

"Waiting to make sure you're okay!" I shot back, hurt turning to anger. "Not everyone approaches human connection as a strategic exercise, Zach. Some of us actually feel things."

The moment the words were out, regret slammed into me. He flinched, the accusation hitting a nerve I hadn't intended to expose so cruelly.

"I shouldn't have come here." He said quietly, turning toward the door.

"Zach, wait." I grabbed his arm, the contact electric. "Don't leave. Please."

He froze, tense beneath my touch, neither pulling away nor facing me again. The air between us vibrated with unspoken accusations and fragile feelings.

"What do you want from me, Theo?" His voice was low, ragged. "The CTO's perspective on algorithmic anomalies? The CEO's statement on security breaches? Or something else entirely?"

His pain cut through my anger, leaving only a raw ache. "I want the truth. Not as a journalist. As whatever we are to each other now."

Something shifted in his stance. He moved

toward my window, gazing out at the city, his shoulders slumped with exhaustion.

"The security breach was orchestrated. Deliberately leaked."

"And the algorithm?"

He turned back, meeting my eyes. "The anomaly Riley identified. The one you saw on my screen. It's real. Less significant than we initially feared, but real."

"And you think I'm going to write about it?" At least I understood the core of his withdrawal. "That I'll use it against you?"

"I haven't been avoiding you." Frustration filled his voice again. "I've been trying to protect LoveLogic's IPO while addressing multiple corporate crises, one of which involves our relationship being exploited for publicity."

"You think I arranged the video leak?" The thought was incredulous, insulting.

"No." He took off his glasses, pinching the bridge of his nose. "But the timing benefits your book. Critic falls for subject makes a compelling narrative."

His perspective, seen through the lens of his history with Marco, made a painful kind of sense. He expected betrayal.

"Zach." I stepped closer, needing him to believe me. "Look at me. I need you to hear this. I don't want to exploit this. I turned down interviews today. Ignored tips about the algorithm. I'm not pursuing this story."

He studied me, eyes searching, a deep weariness in them. "That contradicts your professional interests."

"Yes." I held his gaze, pouring every ounce of sincerity I possessed into the simple word. "It does. Because my personal interests—you—have become more important."

The admission hung between us, raw and irrevocable.

"What exactly are you saying, Theo?" His voice was barely a whisper, suspicion receding.

"I'm saying I could have pursued this story. But I didn't. Because whatever this is—whatever exists between you and me—matters more than a headline. More than the book I thought I was writing."

He remained silent, processing my words with that deliberate intensity I knew so well.

"The algorithm anomaly will be publicly disclosed tomorrow," he said finally. "Full transparency. It affects about three percent of matches, including ours, but doesn't invalidate the core compatibility patterns."

"You're telling me this before the public announcement. Why?"

"Because I trust you. Despite corporate counsel advising against it. Despite the professional risks. I trust you, Theo."

The tension in my chest unraveled. Without conscious thought, I closed the remaining distance, my hands finding his face, pulling him to me as I kissed him with an urgency born of fear, relief, and undeniable need.

He responded instantly, arms wrapping around me, anchoring me as the kiss deepened. Whatever boundaries we'd maintained dissolved, swept aside by the raw hunger driving us now.

"I've missed you," I murmured against his mouth.

His hands tightened at my waist. "It's only been a couple of days."

"Felt longer." I fumbled with his tie needing to remove it. "For the record, I trust you, too. Even when it complicates everything."

"It does complicate everything." His mouth found the sensitive skin below my ear, his touch sending shivers down my spine as tension simmered between us. "Professionally speaking, this is highly inadvisable."

"Incredibly inadvisable." Heat rushed my words as I fumbled with his buttons. "Completely incompatible with objective journalism."

"Significant conflict of interest." His voice was rough as my fingers found the smooth skin of his chest. "Ethically questionable at best."

"We should probably stop, then." I made no move to pull away.

"Logically, yes." His hands slid beneath my t-shirt, cool against me, and short-circuited rational thought. "Though I find my interest in logical behavior significantly diminished at present."

A shaky laugh escaped me. "Did you just admit that Zach Mendez, logic incarnate, isn't feeling particularly logical?"

His lips found mine again, a ghost of a smile against my mouth. "Though I prefer to think of it as prioritizing research over theory."

"Is that what we're doing? Research?" I pulled back just enough to see his face, needing clarity amidst the rising tide of sensation.

"No." All traces of humor vanished, replaced by an intensity that stole my breath. "This has nothing to do with research, algorithms, or publicity arrangements. This is only us, Theo. Nothing else."

The simple assertion, the quiet certainty in his expression—it anchored me.

"Only us," I echoed.

Zach lifted my shirt and I raised my arms so he could slip it off. It dropped onto the floor behind me.

He cupped my face with unexpected tenderness, those brilliant eyes studying me with an intensity that left me simultaneously exposed and desired.

"Let's go get comfortable."

He nodded and gave a shy smile. I took his hand, lacing our fingers together, and led him toward my bedroom.

Zach stopped me at the door as uncertainty clouded his expression.

"What is it?" I asked.

"I haven't done this in... a while," he admitted, an uncharacteristic hesitation. "Not with someone who matters."

My heart constricted at his words. "It's okay. Neither have I."

I quickly got his shirt off and traced the lean lines of his torso, noticing the slight tremor beneath my fingertips giving away his nervousness. Or maybe it was excitement? When I looked up, his expression was naked with wanting.

"You're beautiful," he murmured, hands hovering at my waist.

His caress was deliberate, exploratory, the precision that defined his life translating into an exquisite attentiveness that left me breathless. The same man who built a tech empire from code focused all that careful attention on me, cataloging every reaction, learning what made my breath catch.

"These clothes have got to go," I said.

We pulled apart just enough to shed shoes and pants, our breaths fast and uneven. When we reached our underwear, we paused. Zach's eyes met mine as he stepped closer, sliding his hand down the waistband of my boxers and cupping me through the fabric.

"I've thought about this since our first kiss." He brushed his thumb across the damp cotton, and my cock throbbed in response.

I swallowed hard and took a step back to slide them down. I watched, unmoving, as his eyes roamed over me.

"It's your turn," I said, barely above a whisper.

Zach hesitated a beat, then hooked his thumbs into the waistband of his briefs and pushed them down. We stood there, taking each other in, the air between us humming with anticipation. He was stunning, his dick thick and with a drop of precum at the tip.

I stepped forward, and our cocks touched. I wrapped a hand around both of us, thrilling the pulse of his arousal against mine. Our lips met again, hungrier now. I stroked us together, as we moaned through the kisses.

"Tell me what you like," he whispered against the sensitive hollow of my neck, his warm breath sending delicious shivers down my spine.

"You. Just keep touching me... please don't stop."

We tumbled onto the bed in a tangle of limbs, skin against heated skin. No barriers left, only desperate need. He was methodical—but now he applied that precision to pleasure, treating my body as if it were a code to crack, leaving me trembling, whimpering beneath him.

"Is this good?" he asked, voice low and tight with barely maintained restraint.

"God, yes!" I clutched at his broad shoulders.

Something cracked open in his expression as desire overtook him. He kissed me desperately, passionately, as though he could pour everything he couldn't articulate into the connection between us.

We moved together, finding a rhythm that was thrillingly new and made my pulse race. When Zach broke the kiss, there was a fire in his eyes. He eased me onto my back.

His mouth traveled down my body. Each press of his lips and nibble expertly placed to draw out the strongest response. I lost myself in the sensations he created—with every stroke of his tongue, every teasing pull.

"Oh, Zach." I managed between moans. "You're

incredible." As he sucked on one nipple and tweaked another with his fingers, pleasure shot through me, stealing my voice for a moment. "It doesn't seem like you're out of practice," I finally said.

"I'm. Glad. You. Think. So." The words were punctuated by kisses that he peppered down my stomach.

Tension and anticipation built as he teased and explored. He paused at my dick, looking between it and me. I looked back at him. He was on all fours next to me, his perfect ass in the air. My erection bounced, demanding attention. But he didn't move. He raised an eyebrow as he smiled.

I nodded.

He returned the acknowledgement with a wider grin.

He spread my legs wide, settling between them like he belonged there. His erection bobbed with his every move, thick and hard. I wanted it, but even more I wanted to know what he planned to do to me.

Then he bent low and licked a slow, searing line from the base of my balls all the way to the tip of my cock. It was a white-hot stripe of pleasure that reverberated through my body.

"Holy fuck!" I slapped my hand on the bed as my hips lifted, needing more of him. Of his mouth.

He didn't hesitate. Locking his lips around my

shaft, he worked me deep into his throat with a level of skill and control that left me breathless.

Zach's lips and tongue moved in perfect sync, bringing me to the edge, then pulling back, keeping me on that precarious brink. Each touch, each movement, heightened the sensations. The intensity was almost too much to bear. Tremors ran through my body, the need for release growing more urgent.

He held me right there for so long it felt like torture—delicious, maddening torment that rewired my whole body with want. Every time I looked at him, his eyes met mine—daring me to let go. It was a battle of wills, a test of endurance, and one that I was close to losing.

Finally, with a slight increase in pressure and a flick of his tongue, there was no stopping it.

"Zach. Zach. Oh. I'm cumming."

He gave a muffled "uh-huh" as the orgasm tore through me. He kept sucking and with each movement increased the intensity. I couldn't hold back the raw, primal groans, proof of just how powerful that climax was. He swallowed every drop.

As I came down from the high, Zach's eyes were filled with a mixture of satisfaction and triumph. He seemed pleased to have brought me such intense pleasure. It was a side of him I had never seen before, and it left me exhilarated and utterly undone.

He crawled up my body and planted a slow, scorching kiss on me that wracked me with more shudders. He thrust against me, hard and leaking.

"Your turn," I murmured against his mouth, my hands already roaming over his body.

Zach shook his head, a slight smile tugging at the corner of his mouth. "You don't have to—"

"I want to." I reached between us and wrapped my fingers around him. A low groan escaped him as I began to stroke him. "I need to."

He adjusted, sitting up and pinning my spent cock under his ass to give me better access. So much slick leaked from him I didn't need lube. Rock hard, with his balls already drawn tight, he wasn't going to last long.

He pulsed hot and urgent in my grip. I watched his face, the way his lips parted, his breath ragged as I changed the rhythm of my strokes.

His eyes fluttered closed as I quickened my pace. His breath caught and held, body drawn tight as I pushed him closer and closer. Heat radiated from him, the desperation in his every movement. Watching Zach unravel under my touch—this man who was usually so composed—was intensely satisfying.

"Theo," he gasped, his hands gripping at my hips. "I can't—I won't last—"

I kept my pace even, savoring the way his body responded to every stroke, every twist of my wrist.

"Don't hold back," I urged, my voice low and steady. "Let go, Zach."

His body shuddered, his release spilled over my hand, streaking my stomach and chest.

"Oh, fuck yes." My words mixed with his moans as I continued to stroke him until he had nothing left.

I brought my hand to my lips and tasted him, earning another moan as I looked up at his blissed-out face.

"That was…" he began, then paused, searching for the right word.

I smiled against his shoulder, trying to think of the most perfect Zach word. "Ineffable?"

A soft laugh escaped him as he shifted to lie beside me. "I was going to say 'unquantifiable.' But yes."

I caressed his hip, feeling the goosebumps rise in response. "The great Zach Mendez, at a loss for metrics."

His expression sobered as he brushed hair from my forehead with gentle fingers. "There are some things that defy measurement."

I pressed closer, savoring the warmth of him.

"What happens tomorrow?" I asked, reality intruding despite my best efforts to keep it at bay.

I shrugged. "We'll figure it out. Later." He rolled on to his side to face me. "For tonight, let's just focus on us. Maybe we could start with a shower?"

I nodded. I hadn't expected that answer. It said a lot he wasn't going back into work mode, that he was letting this moment continue.

"And then some dinner." I kissed him, looking forward to whatever else an evening together might bring.

18

Zach

I'D BEEN awake for hours, staring at the unfamiliar ceiling. Beside me, Theo slept, his breathing deep and steady, one arm thrown carelessly across my chest. The weight comforted me, even as dread coiled in my gut.

He had trusted me with everything last night—his body, his words, his heart. But I hadn't given him the full truth in return. Not yet.

My phone on the nightstand vibrated with notifications I knew were piling up—Trina, Riley, corporate counsel.

Today was the day we disclosed the algorithm anomaly. But before that firestorm, I had to navigate this personal one. How could I tell him? How could I explain that our match wasn't some random glitch? It was a feature born from my deepest hurt. Designed to find the kind of connection that defied conventional logic. A connection like ours.

The professional implications were manageable—transparency, mitigation, revised projections.

The personal implications felt catastrophic.

Theo had built his entire critique on the dangers of algorithmic manipulation. His family history was a testament to the damage systems like mine could inflict. How could he see this as anything but the ultimate betrayal? My defenses—once so solid—had collapsed because of our connection. And now they couldn't shield me from what came next.

A soft sigh beside me. Theo stirred, nuzzling closer before his eyes blinked open, focusing on me with drowsy warmth.

"Morning." His voice was thick with sleep. A slow smile spread across his face, erasing any lingering grogginess. "I should have known you were an early riser."

"Force of habit." My voice sounded stiff.

He stretched, arching his back with a grace that disrupted my train of thought. "Is there coffee in that contemplative stare, or do I need to make some?"

He started to slide out of bed, casual and completely at ease in his skin—and my being there—

in a way that twisted the knot of anxiety tighter in my stomach.

"Stay," I said. The word was sharper than intended. "I'll do it. Then we need to talk."

His teasing smile faded, replaced by that keen, analytical focus I knew so well. He sank back against the pillows, pulling the sheet higher, watching me. "Okay."

I extracted myself carefully and put on my pants and shirt from last night, needing to wear more than just briefs. Moving to his kitchen, going through the motions of making coffee—grinding beans, measuring water—provided a temporary distraction.

"Is this about the algorithm disclosure today?" he called out.

"Partly." I returned with two mugs, handing one to him before perching on the edge of the bed. For a moment I couldn't take my eyes off him sitting against the headboard, shirtless, taking the first sip. I forced myself to focus. "There are details about the anomaly I didn't fully explain last night."

Theo took another drink, his eyes never leaving my face. "What details?"

I drew a breath, holding his gaze. "The pattern recognition module—the one that flagged our match—contains a weighting bias. We know that."

"Potential inflation of twelve to fifteen percent."

He confirmed. "Making us high seventies instead of low nineties."

"Yes." My throat went dry. More coffee didn't help. "But I need to explain why that bias exists. It's not a random coding error." I paused, gathering the words. "I built it to identify complementary traits in personalities that don't seem compatible. It seeks out patterns where surface-level opposition might mask deeper alignment. In rare cases, like ours, it turns out the weights impact the score even more. That last part... it's not supposed to do that."

Theo froze, the mug halfway to his lips. I watched the pieces connect behind his eyes—the journalist, the critic, the man I slept with last night—all converging on the implications of my confession.

"You built it." His voice was unnervingly quiet. "Based on your experience with Marco."

The rawness of his perception cut straight to the core. It was both terrifying and, in a strange way, a relief. No deflection was possible.

"Yes." I took a breath and when he said nothing I continued. "I wanted to create a system that could identify authentic connection potential beneath surface differences. Prevent the pain that comes from misinterpreting compatibility."

He set his mug down on the nightstand, the small clink echoing in the silence. Then he pulled the sheet higher, covering himself, creating a physical barrier. When he spoke again, his voice had cooled several degrees. His analytical edge returned in full force. "So, our match wasn't just influenced by a technical anomaly. It resulted from a pattern recognition system you designed based on your personal trauma, specifically programmed to find connections like ours."

"That's a harsh interpretation."

"Is it inaccurate?" His gaze was sharp, probing.

"The system identified genuine complementary patterns between us." I struggled to keep the defensiveness from my voice. "The anomaly isn't that it found compatibility where none exists. It's that it weighted certain complementary traits more heavily than intended because of that specific design focus."

"Traits you designed it to prioritize because of your past." He swung his legs out of bed, standing and pulling on his jeans, turning his back to me. What we'd shared last night felt like a distant memory. "So, the algorithm matched you with its fiercest critic—someone embodying exactly the opposition you programmed it to look for."

"That's an oversimplification. The system didn't manufacture anything. What's developed between us isn't an algorithmic creation."

"Isn't it?" He turned, crossing his arms. "Your

algorithm matched us at 92% because you coded it to seek out the oppositional dynamic we represent. The publicity arrangement forced you and me together, despite those oppositions. Our entire relationship originated from, and was sustained by, your technological intervention."

I stood abruptly, needing to counter his accusation and bridge the widening gap between us. "The algorithm created opportunity. Everything since—our conversations, the arguments, the connection, last night—that was us, Theo. Not the code."

"Was it?" His voice dropped lower, and the vulnerability broke through his argumentative tone. "Or was it the product of enough forced proximity that even opposing worldviews found a way to adapt? Stockholm syndrome for intellectual adversaries?"

The phrase landed like a physical blow, striking at the heart of my fragile belief in the authenticity of what we'd had. "Do you actually believe that? After everything?"

He ran a hand through his already tousled hair, turning away again to pace the small space between the bed and the window. "I don't know what to believe anymore, Zach! I know how I feel when I'm with you. But I also know those emotions were potentially engineered by a system you designed to find connections that wouldn't naturally emerge."

"Nothing about how I feel for you was engineered." I hoped my honesty would pierce his arguments. "The algorithm didn't create my feelings. They exist independently of any code."

"But it created the conditions for them to develop!" He spun back to face me, his eyes flashing with a mixture of pain and anger. "Don't you see? This is the ultimate validation of my critique! These systems go beyond identifying compatibility. They manufacture it through technological intervention. And I'm the perfect case study!"

"Stop analyzing this like a journalist!" I shot back. "This isn't a story or a data point! It's us!"

"Is there an *us* outside the algorithm?" The question hung in the air, heavy with desperation beneath its challenge. "Would you have ever chosen me—the guy publicly dissecting your life's work—without your system overriding conventional logic and telling you we were compatible?"

"Yes." The answer was immediate. "But we might never have discovered that compatibility without the initial match facilitating the interaction."

Theo slammed his hand against the windowsill, startling me with the sudden violence of the gesture. "And that is the fundamental problem! These systems don't just identify potential—they alter destiny! They create connections that fate, or choice, or whatever you want to call organic human interaction, wouldn't have arranged!"

"You're projecting your parents' situation onto us." I hit his pain point deliberately. "You're so terrified of repeating history, of being manipulated by technology, that you can't trust any connection technology touches. You're looking for flaws to validate your pre-existing critique."

"And you're so terrified of vulnerability, so determined to control human connection through logic because of Marco, you can't see how your trauma shaped the very system that brought us together. You manufactured this!"

"I manufactured nothing! The algorithm doesn't control emotions. It doesn't create desire! It identifies potential compatibility patterns—patterns that are real between us, whether or not you want to admit it!"

"There's a circularity here. A feedback loop created by your past. How can I trust that what I feel isn't just... noise in your system? Proof that your biased code works exactly as intended?"

"And how can I trust that you're not rejecting the truth of what we've built because acknowledging it would invalidate your entire professional stance?" I further weaponized his own conflict against him, even as I hated doing it. "Maybe the truth is you can't handle that we're genuinely compatible despite our differences, and the algorithm simply saw it first."

We stood facing each other, the remnants of last night—rumpled sheets, clothes on the floor—a mocking backdrop to the wreckage we were creating.

"Where does this leave us?" I asked after he'd been quiet for too long.

Theo looked at me, the anger draining from his expression, leaving behind a profound weariness that mirrored my own. "I think," he said slowly, "it leaves us exactly where we started. You believing technology can enhance human connection, while I see it as fundamentally altering it in problematic ways."

"That's a philosophical position. I'm asking about us. Personally."

He moved toward where his shirt lay on the floor, avoiding my eyes. "I think I need time. To figure out what's real and what's a data point in your trauma-informed algorithm."

The clinical phrasing, the deliberate distancing— he might as well have slammed a door in my face. "And the dinner? The final date?"

"We should cancel it." Theo pulled his shirt on. "Any further public performance would be pointless."

He was right, logically and professionally. "And that's it?" I struggled to keep my voice even. "We just... end things?"

"We're not ending anything that wasn't artificially constructed to begin with."

The words, denying the reality of everything that had passed between us since that first confrontation, landed with brutal precision.

He didn't believe in it. In us.

I wanted to argue, to list the moments that transcended any app. But I saw the conviction in his stance, the retreat into intellectual defense as a shield against emotional risk. He clung to that narrative to maintain his worldview.

"Fine." I retreated to the safety of professional detachment. "We should coordinate messaging regarding the publicity experiment's conclusion."

He nodded, pain crossing his features before his composure returned. "I'll have Vivian contact your team. For what it's worth," he added, his voice was barely audible, "I don't regret getting to know the real you, Zach. Whatever caused that to happen."

I quickly gathered the rest of my things and left while he looked out the window.

Outside Theo's apartment, my phone continued to buzz, demanding attention.

LoveLogic waited, expecting the focus and precision I was known for.

But standing there, I confronted a truth more devastating than any corporate crisis. The system I'd built to predict and facilitate human connection had utterly failed to account for the complexities of the human heart.

Especially my own.

In prioritizing logic over vulnerability, certainty over trust, I might have jeopardized the most significant connection I'd ever found.

19

Theo

THE BLINKING CURSOR WAS A TINY, persistent heartbeat on the otherwise dead screen.

Three hours I'd sat here, trying to channel the raw, jagged edges of my confusion and hurt into the righteous anger Vivian wanted. Into the sharp critique the publisher expected.

My fingers moved in an attempt at productivity.

*LoveLogic's recent disclosure of algorithmic anomalies confirms what critics have long suspected: these systems, built on flawed human assumptions, create a false sense of scientific certainty while concealing fundamental biases...*

I pictured Zach's face as he'd explained the anomaly—the exhaustion, the vulnerability beneath the technical explanation. *Flawed human assumptions.* The phrase was... yuck.

Delete.

*The revelation that LoveLogic's founder designed his compatibility algorithm based on personal relationship trauma raises profound ethical questions. Can a system meant to prevent one kind of pain inadvertently inflict another, manipulating connection itself...*

*Manipulation.* Had it felt like manipulation when Zach listened, truly listened, to my mother? When his hand found mine in the darkness of that diner?

Delete.

*When technology attempts to predict human compatibility, it inevitably reflects the biases and wounds of its creators. Zach Mendez's algorithm, designed to find complementary opposition based on a betrayal he experienced, transformed personal trauma into systemic influence, making the match between creator and critic not an anomaly, but an inevitability...*

*Inevitability.* The word wasn't right. Nothing about the chaotic, unpredictable path from that first confrontation to kissing him in my apartment was inevitable. It was more a series of unexpected choices, moments of colliding orbits.

I slammed the laptop shut and shoved my hands through my hair, pacing across the worn rug while Zach's words churned relentlessly in my head.

I was stuck on what I said to him.

*Stockholm syndrome for ideological adversaries.*

*These systems don't just identify potential—they alter destiny*

My phone buzzed, and I glanced at the screen.

Vivian: *Manuscript deadline approaching. Progress update?*

I was regressing, trapped in yet another feedback loop. I couldn't honestly write the old critique. But acknowledging the complexity felt like a professional betrayal, a concession that maybe the algorithm wasn't entirely wrong.

Ignoring the text, I grabbed my jacket and keys, needing air, space, and perspective. I walked without direction. People rushed by, eyes locked on their screens. Some were oblivious. Some, perhaps, had just been matched—by LoveLogic, trusting the heart-shaped logo of Zach's creation. A creation that I now knew was born from his deepest hurt.

Was that the story? The wounded creator embedding his trauma into the code? It felt too simple, too neat. Too much like the takedown narrative I no longer believed.

An hour later, almost without conscious navigation, I stood on my mother's porch. Warm garlic and herbs spilled from the house like an embrace—rich, nostalgic, and uncomplicated. Exactly what I needed. She opened the door wearing paint-splattered overalls over a turtleneck, reading glasses perched on her nose.

"This is a surprise." Her perceptive gaze took in my disheveled state before I'd even uttered a word. "Though your timing is excellent. I just finished making soup."

The familiar comfort of her kitchen wrapped around me. She filled two bowls, setting one before me without asking if I was hungry. She always knew what I needed.

"You look terrible." She settled opposite me, her expression a blend of maternal concern and clinical assessment. "I assume this has to do with the canceled dinner at Veritas and the rather vague press statement about 'concluding the compatibility experiment by mutual agreement.'"

"You're following what the press is saying?"

"I follow anything concerning my son and the algorithm man." She studied me over her glasses. "Though I notice you haven't said much about either. Vivian says you're struggling with the manuscript."

"The manuscript is fine." I lied, focusing on my

food and avoiding her eyes. "Just... refining the argument."

Her raised eyebrow conveyed eloquent disbelief. "Theodore James Barrett. I recognize avoidance patterns when I see them. You're circling the issue like a nervous grad student defending a shaky thesis."

The soup was grounding, its warmth a contrast to the chill of my thoughts. "It's complicated." I managed finally, the understatement coiled tight in my chest.

"Relationships usually are." Her voice was gentle. "Especially when they challenge our carefully constructed worldviews." She used my words against me.

"It wasn't a relationship." I mumbled, the denial automatic. "It was a publicity stunt that went off the rails."

"Mmm." There was her infuriatingly perceptive hum. "And did it go 'off the rails' before or after discovering his code was designed to identify connections like yours?"

I set my spoon down, the clatter sharp. "Vivian has been thorough."

"Vivian's concerned." She paused and held my gaze. "So am I. You've avoided talking about what happened. You look like you haven't slept. And you're clearly blocked trying to write about it. What's really going on here?"

Maybe she was right. Maybe I needed to voice the conflict, not just wrestle with it internally. I told her everything about why Zach developed the algorithm like he did.

She listened patiently, even as I restated parts she'd already heard.

"Doesn't that prove my whole point?" I asked once I'd explained it all. The question felt raw, ripped from the heart of my conflict. "That these systems don't just find compatibility, they engineer it? If we only connected because his code sought someone like me, isn't that the ultimate example of technology distorting authentic choice?"

My mother considered this, her expression thoughtful. "That's one interpretation," she said after what seemed like an eternity. "Though I find it interesting that in rejecting Zach because of how you were matched, you seem to be reinforcing the algorithm's power over human choice."

I stared at her, blindsided. "What?"

"If you walk away from a connection you value simply because of how you discovered its potential, you're letting the algorithm dictate your choice just as surely as if you'd blindly followed its initial suggestion." She remained calm as she shared her point of view. "Either way, technology determines the outcome, not your own judgment or feelings."

The paradox struck me, sharp and disorienting.

Had I done that? Had I rejected something that might be real because its origin felt artificial? Did that mean I was just as susceptible to the algorithm's influence as my father had been?

"That's..." I faltered. "It feels different."

"Of course it does. You developed genuine feelings for Zach Mendez. And acknowledging the emotional truth requires revising your professional narrative and confronting your own fears about repeating your father's mistakes."

Her words exposed the tangled knot of my identity as a critic and personal anxieties. Was I rejecting Zach to protect my critique? To protect myself from the potential pain of a connection that was complicated?

"Even if that were true, the circularity remains. He programmed it to find us."

"Life is full of patterns." Her voice was calm but carried an authority that steadied me. "We all create systems reflecting our experiences—technological, theoretical, emotional. Your father used psychological theory to justify leaving. I researched attachment while partnering with someone avoidant. We seek what we know, even unconsciously." She reached across the table and placed her hand on mine. "The algorithm created an opportunity, Theo. It revealed a potential pattern. What happened next, was that authentic? Was that human? Only you can answer that."

I left her house hours later, my head clearer, but my conflict unresolved.

---

I COULDN'T AVOID my meeting with Vivian. It was an inevitable confrontation I needed to get through. *The Fulcrum's* offices were sleek, intimidating, a world away from my mother's comforting kitchen.

Vivian was once again at her desk with a printed copy of the manuscript spread before her.

"Finally." She gestured to the chair. "I was starting to draft a missing person's report."

The weight of professional expectation settled the moment I sat down. "I needed perspective."

"Your new angle seems to have resulted in... this." She tapped the pages. "These chapters are fighting themselves. Half scathing critique, half reluctant admiration for the complexity of the system and its creator. It's intellectual whiplash."

She wasn't wrong. My writing mirrored my internal state—fragmented, contradictory, afraid to commit to a single truth. "I'm trying to integrate new information," I said weakly.

Vivian leaned back, studying me. "Theo, when this started, I expected insider access to strengthen your critique. I didn't expect it to fundamentally change your perspective. So, what book are you actually writing now? Because this halfway nonsense isn't working."

"I don't know anymore." It was a relief to admit it. Even if it struck me like failure. "After everything I've been through, the book I signed on to write no longer rings entirely true."

"Which is?"

"That technology doesn't necessarily prevent authentic connection. It creates opportunities. The algorithm showed potential between Zach and me—potential we might have missed because of our differences. But what happened next? That wasn't engineered. That was human choice."

She nodded slowly, processing. "And you walked away from that connection because acknowledging its authenticity complicates this." She tapped the manuscript again.

Her observation echoed my mother's. I wondered if she had already told Vivian everything—if they'd been talking since I left her house. "I walked away because I needed to figure out whether the bond was real or just an algorithmic artifact."

"And have you figured it out?"

Our argument came to mind. Zach's willingness to face critique. The warmth beneath all his logic. The gut-wrenching grief I hadn't shaken. I chose my words carefully before continuing.

"I think I used valid intellectual concerns as a shield against emotional risk. Rejecting Zach allowed me to maintain my critical stance, yes." Another pause. I wasn't sure I wanted to say what was on my mind. But at this point, what did I have to lose? "Maybe it was also safer than trusting a connection that defied easy categorization."

Understanding crossed Vivian's face. "So, what are you going to do?"

The decision suddenly seemed crystal clear. "I need to write the truth as I understand it now. A book that explores the complexities—the risks and the potential benefits of these systems."

"The publisher wanted a takedown," Vivian reminded me.

"Then they can reject it." It surprised me how comfortable I was with that statement. "I won't compromise the truth of my experience for a contract."

"And personally?"

The question hung in the air.

"I don't know yet," I admitted. "But the first step is acknowledging the truth in my writing. Getting honest with myself."

Vivian gathered the manuscript pages. "Then rewrite it. All of it. Stop hedging. Write what you believe." She dumped the stack of papers into her trashcan. "And Theo?" Her voice held a less sharp tone. "Whatever happens with Mendez personal honesty usually aligns with professional integrity in the long run. Trust that."

BACK IN MY apartment that night, the blinking cursor invited me to write. Words began to flow, not easily, but with a clarity that had been missing for days.

*The journey from skeptic to nuanced observer is rarely linear, particularly when the subject of one's critique becomes the catalyst for personal evolution. Algorithmic matchmaking systems present undeniable ethical challenges, yet direct engagement reveals a more complex reality: technology creates opportunities, but humans create connection. The algorithm may identify patterns, but the choice to engage, to risk vulnerability, to build something meaningful despite differences—that remains profoundly, uniquely human...*

I wrote for hours, weaving together critique and complexity, acknowledging the validity of my initial concerns while integrating the unexpected truths I'd discovered through knowing Zach. The manuscript emerging wasn't the one I'd planned, but it was honest in a way the original never was.

I wasn't sure if Zach would ever want to see me again. But I knew now that I wanted the chance to tell him the truth—not just in writing, but in person.

# 20

Zach

Each display in LoveLogic's algorithm development lab revealed different aspects of the pattern recognition module we'd been analyzing. The space was usually full of developers, but now only Riley and Dr. Elena Kostas, the behavioral psychologist who consulted on our earliest compatibility metrics, remained.

I'd worked here for most of the day, dissecting the module I knew better than my own apartment layout.

This wasn't just about code integrity anymore. It was about Theo.

My fingers flew across the keyboard, initiating another simulation run. Variation twelve.

If the core compatibility was an illusion—a ghost generated by a biased machine—what did that make everything that had happened between us? I stood and paced the length of the room, the polished floor reflecting the glow of the screens.

Six months ago, this anomaly would have registered purely as a technical challenge. Now I was digging at the foundation of something fragile and essential.

Riley, hunched over his own terminal nearby, looked up. "Variation twelve complete, Zach."

I returned to my seat to review the outcome, forcing my focus through the fog of personal anxiety.

Dr. Kostas observed from her position near the whiteboard. Her composed presence was a stark contrast to my internal turmoil.

I scanned the results. The programmer in me traced the correlation patterns, methodical and detached as always. But the rest of me—the part that had held Theo's hand, heard his laughter, seen the pain beneath his critique—searched for something else. Something more than data. Something that might explain how an algorithm could lead to a connection that felt real.

"Eighty-seven percent," I murmured, the revised compatibility score was higher but still not the previous ninety-two. "Even with the weighting bias completely removed."

"Still well above our threshold for highly compatible matches," Riley confirmed, a hint of vindication in his voice as the data was proving the system's foundation sound.

Dr. Kostas moved closer to the display. "This pattern holds across all variations, Zach. The initial ninety-two percent may have been slightly inflated by the weighting, but the core compatibility indicators remain remarkably consistent. The underlying patterns are strong."

I turned to face her, needing more than technical validation. "What does that mean, Elena? In lay terms."

Her gaze was direct but gentle. "It means that you and Mr. Barrett possess genuinely complementary traits that the algorithm correctly identified. The system didn't manufacture compatibility where none existed—it recognized patterns that might not be obvious but are demonstrably real. The initial score was slightly off, but the reason why you matched holds true."

Recognition. Not manufacturing.

The distinction settled over me, not with the triumph I might have expected even a few weeks ago, but instead with a glimmer of hope that maybe something could be salvaged. The anomaly hadn't created a false positive. Instead, it had simply overemphasized elements of compatibility that were present.

"Which aspects stand out to you?" I pressed, needing to understand the mechanics of us as the algorithm saw it.

"Several are striking." She gestured toward a specific data cluster on the screen. "Despite significant philosophical differences, you share similar core values around authenticity, intellectual integrity, and the pursuit of meaningful connection. Your communication styles are distinct but highly complementary. Your precision balances his intuitive style, creating what we call 'constructive tension.' The very thing that likely drew you into those intense debates."

She pointed to another cluster. "Most interesting is this pattern here—cognitive processing complementarity. You both engage deeply with complex problems but approach them from different frameworks that, when combined, create more comprehensive solutions than either would reach independently."

Understanding crystallized, sharp and clear. "That's what the algorithm detected. Not just compatibility despite our differences, but because of them." This wasn't all based on the limitations I'd written into the system out of fear. It was an evolution shaped collectively by the LoveLogic team over time.

"Precisely." Her confirmation came with a small smile. "Your different perspectives don't inherently spark conflict—they create completion. It's quite elegant, actually. The algorithm saw the potential for synergy beneath the surface friction."

The lab door hissed open, shattering the focused atmosphere. Daniel Park strode in, his movements radiating impatience and controlled fury. His gaze swept past Riley and Dr. Kostas, landing squarely on me.

"I've been looking for you. The emergency investor call is in twenty minutes. We need to finalize our position on the publicity disaster."

"I'm in the middle of critical algorithm analysis." I gestured toward the screens, annoyance tightening my jaw.

Daniel's eyes narrowed. "This obsession with the pattern recognition module needs to end. The compatibility experiment is over. Barrett has returned to his predictable critique. The algorithm's technical specifications are irrelevant to our current crisis, which is managing the perception that our founder got played by a journalist."

"That's where you're wrong." I defended the

algorithm like I was defending the potential of what Theo and I had found. "We have to understand its exact functionality to address both the technical disclosure and the public narrative. We lead with integrity, not damage control."

Riley and Dr. Kostas exchanged uneasy glances.

Daniel moved closer, lowering his voice to a clipped whisper. "This isn't about investors or analytics anymore, is it? This is about Barrett. Your judgment is compromised."

I met his gaze, prepared to do battle—a shift of tactic influenced by Theo challenging my assumptions. "This is about understanding what my system actually detected, because that insight affects everything from our technical disclosure to our public messaging. It's about the integrity of the science."

"Your personal feelings toward our critic have clouded your judgment." Daniel's voice was as cold as I'd ever heard it. "The board is concerned."

That phrase didn't have the impact on me that it used to. "They should be focused on accurate technical disclosure and the ethical handling of user data, not on suppressing key information." Theo's arguments echoed in my words.

Daniel studied me for a long moment, resentment flashing behind his eyes. "The investor call will proceed with or without you, Zach. I suggest you prioritize appropriately."

He turned and left, the silence in his wake heavier than before. Riley returned to his terminal, while Dr. Kostas observed me.

"This data." I faced the screens again, the confrontation solidifying my strategy. "Compile it. Comprehensive findings, including the complementary trait analysis methodology. Prepare it for publication."

Riley blinked in surprise. "That's proprietary information we've never disclosed."

"It's time we did. User trust requires understanding, not just results. That's the ethical path."

As I gathered my materials for the investor call, Dr. Kostas touched my arm lightly. "The algorithm identified potential compatibility between you and Mr. Barrett. But what developed afterward wasn't algorithmic—it was human choice, engagement, vulnerability. Perhaps that's the distinction that matters most."

Her words sharpened my determination.

The system had opened a door, presented data. But Theo and I had walked through it.

"Thank you, Elena. Your insight has been invaluable."

Her smile was warm and kind. "I've been

happily married for twenty-five years to someone who looks completely wrong for me on paper. Sometimes the most meaningful connections defy straightforward analysis."

---

THE INVESTOR CALL WAS GRUELING. Ninety minutes of navigating concern, suspicion, and pressure to prioritize optics over substance. I held firm, advocating for full transparency, emphasizing the underlying strength of algorithms. Daniel repeatedly tried to steer the conversation back to market projections, but I refused to downplay the technical results.

Afterward, Daniel confronted me again. His voice barely contained his anger. "You prioritized the wrong messaging. The board has another meeting tomorrow. We'll be discussing whether your leadership aligns with our pre-IPO strategy."

The threat, once capable of triggering intense anxiety, had become secondary. "I'll be prepared to explain my approach."

Back in my office, I opened the analysis we'd prepared in the lab. It was a defense, not only of the algorithm, but of the potential for connections like the one I'd found and possibly ruined.

Without second guessing my decision, I attached the document to an email.

*To: Theo Barrett. Subject: Analysis.*

No message, just the data. An act of trust. I offered the raw truth so he could draw his own conclusions.

I completed the public disclosure strategy, embedding the principle of transparency I'd fought for. The work filled the time but not the hollow ache that had settled in my chest since Theo had walked away, leaving me alone with the wreckage of our argument.

Once I accomplished everything needed for tomorrow and emailed it to Trina to spin into marketing-speak, I picked up the small notebook I'd started after the museum visit. Observations sparked by conversations with Theo. Questions challenging my own certainty.

An entry from the night of the poetry reading stood out.

*Connection exists both because of and despite our different frameworks. His intuitive approach finds truths my analytical method misses. My precision clarifies what his intuition discovers. Not opposition —completion.*

I'd written that before I understood how the algorithm's functions had evolved from what I designed—before realizing it had identified exactly this pattern. The realization slammed into me that this entry echoed Dr. Kostas' conclusion.

My logic surrendered to a more essential imperative. I gathered my things, shut down the computer, and left the office.

---

RAIN SOAKED through my jacket as I stood in front of Theo's brownstone. I hesitated before pressing the buzzer. Once. Twice. The silence stretched. Pulling out my phone, my fingers clumsy with cold and anxiety, I typed out a message.

Zach: *I'm outside your building. I need to talk to you. No publicity. No arrangement. Just us.*

Minutes crawled by. Maybe this was a mistake, forcing a confrontation he clearly didn't want. Then, the sharp, welcome buzz unlocked the front door.

The four flights of stairs felt like an ascent toward judgment. What would I say? How could I bridge the gap our argument had created? By the time I reached his landing, breathless, logic had ceded control to the simple need to see him.

Theo opened his apartment door before I could knock. Faded jeans, worn t-shirt, hair endearingly messy. His expression was guarded, wary, but crucially, not closed off.

"You're soaking wet." He stepped back.

"It's raining." I dripped onto his floor.

"I noticed." A ghost of his usual dry humor surfaced. "So, this isn't a scheduled publicity appearance."

"No." I removed my drenched jacket. "This is just me. Wanting to talk to you." I met his eyes, holding his gaze. "Did you read the analysis I sent?"

"I did." He moved to the kitchen, returning with a towel that he handed me. "It was... thorough."

I dried my hair, face, and glasses, gathering thoughts that had seemed clear until this moment standing before him. "The algorithm didn't manufacture compatibility between us. It recognized complementary patterns that might not be immediately obvious but are valid."

"I know. I've been doing some analysis of my own."

"You have?"

"Not with high-tech simulations and behavioral scientists." A slight smile touched his lips. "More the middle-of-the-night, questioning-everything-I-thought-I-knew variety."

The anxiety in my chest loosened.

I needed to address our breaking point directly.

"What I said during our argument about you being intellectually invested in proving our match invalid. That was unfair. And untrue."

"No." Theo's quick response surprised me. "It was actually uncomfortably accurate. I was intellectually invested in maintaining my critique, even at the expense of what was developing between us."

His honesty caught me off guard. I'd prepared for defensiveness, not acknowledgment.

"And I was overinvested in validating the algorithm's accuracy when what matters isn't whether the system's match was technically correct, but what happened afterward."

Theo studied me with those perceptive eyes that had seen through my professional façade from our first meeting. "Why are you here, Zach? Really?"

The question cut to the point. In typical Theo fashion, he sought the core truth.

"Because I miss you." Straightforward honesty seemed necessary. "Because what developed between us matters more than how it began. Because I'd rather have complexity with you than algorithmic certainty without you."

His expression shifted, becoming more relaxed and open. "I've been writing about us. Not the publicity arrangement or the compatibility experiment. But how two people with different perspectives found something real despite those differences."

"Found something genuine." Hope cautiously rose within me. "Not engineered or manufactured."

He moved closer. "I was so afraid of proving my father right—of being influenced by algorithmic suggestion rather than authentic choice—that I rejected something real to maintain my position."

His honesty mirrored my own. For the first time, it didn't feel like we were defending our beliefs. Instead, we were meeting in the middle.

"I developed LoveLogic to help people identify meaningful connections. And then I found connection myself and tried to analyze it into submission rather than just embracing it."

"We're quite a pair." A smile broke through on Theo's face for the first time since I'd arrived. "Both rejecting connection for opposite reasons that somehow turn out to be the same reason."

"Complementary cognitive frameworks creating complete understanding."

"Is that what the scientists call it?" He moved closer still. "I just call it us getting out of our own way."

I reached for him without calculation or analysis, responding to the pull that had been growing since we met.

When our lips met, it wasn't with the desperate heat of our last encounter or the tentative exploration of our first. This kiss was different and simple. It was about choosing each other—complicated, imperfect, real.

His hands found my still-damp shirt, fingers working buttons with determined intent. "You should get out of these wet clothes," he murmured against my mouth.

"Very practical suggestion." I was already tugging at his t-shirt.

"I have my moments of logic." He smiled wide as I pulled the shirt over his head.

We fumbled our way to the bedroom, stripping off clothes as we went. I pushed him playfully down on to the mattress.

I was determined to make this moment last as long as possible. To map him with deliberate attention, learning the rhythm of his responses, the signals his body sent. My desire was to know everything he liked. What would bring him the most pleasure? And God, the pleasure of giving him that—could easily become an addiction.

My lips traced a path along his jawline and then down his neck. His breath hitched as I ventured lower, exploring the contours of his chest, working him until his back arched. The sound alone sent a sharp pulse straight to my cock, tightening the ache I was barely keeping in check.

"Zach—" His fingers twisted in my hair, not guiding, just holding on.

Every gasp, every moan fed into the algorithm of us—rebuilding trust one touch at a time.

I took my time, savoring the way his muscles tensed beneath my hands, how his skin tasted of salt and clean sweat. As I followed the trail below his navel, his body lifted, seeking friction, seeking me.

When I finally took him into my mouth, his gasp punched through the quiet room. Hot and heavy on my tongue, I resisted going too fast. His hips jerked upward before he forced them down, that act of consideration nearly undoing me.

I wanted to devour him, wanted to unravel him thread by thread.

I established a slow, deliberate rhythm, using my hand to explore his balls and caressing the sensitive skin beneath.

"Oh, God—right there—" He clutched at the sheets as his breathing turned ragged. "Zach... so close..."

It was time to change things up.

I pulled off as slowly as I could, holding the head of his cock between my lips before releasing it with a pop.

His breath caught, breaking into a groan of disapproval.

"Where's the lube?" My voice broke, rough with urgency.

"Nightstand," Theo managed to say.

I reached over, yanking the drawer open. The small bottle was half-hidden under a book. I grabbed it and spotted a strip of condoms.

"Condom?" My lips brushed his ear.

"No. Just you. Now."

Those words filled my heart. He didn't hesitate. He was giving himself to me completely—and trusting that I had him. That was sacred, and I'd protect that at all costs.

I positioned myself between his legs and clicked the cap open. He watched as I slicked my fingers.

I pressed against his entrance. He opened beautifully, a low moan spilling from his lips as I worked one finger, then two inside him. He writhed with the tight, hot slide of my touch. I added a third, stretching him gently, watching his face contort in a mix of sharp pleasure and building need.

His eyes flew open, hazy with need as I withdrew.

"Please. Fuck me."

Positioning myself, I slicked my cock while he kept his gaze on me.

Slowly, inch by excruciating inch, I pushed in, loving the way his lips parted, the flutter of his eyelids, the sharp intake of breath before it melted into a groan.

When I was deep inside him, I paused, giving him time to adjust and allow the shockwave of sensation to crest for us. His heat surrounded me, tight and perfect.

"Okay?" I managed, my control fraying.

He nodded, biting his lower lip. "Move." He pled. "You've got to move."

I started with grinding thrusts designed to hit the spot, to make his entire body jolt and his breath stall. I watched him like a hawk, cataloging every gasp, every whimper, every clench of his muscles around me. Learning what made his spine arch, toes curl against my calves, and made his fingers dig into my shoulders hard enough to leave marks.

I wanted those marks.

"Faster?" I asked, though I already knew the answer.

"Yes—God—don't stop—"

I picked up speed, but kept it deliberate, so it would last until I decided to take him completely apart. Every time he got close, teetering on that edge, I changed the angle, slowed down, deepened the thrust just so. He cursed, he begged, he whimpered my name.

"Look at me," I demanded, when his eyes clamped shut.

The raw vulnerability when he focused his gaze on me—his complete surrender—ignited something primal. My climax coiled, a tight spring ready to release, but I pushed it down again.

Not yet.

Not while he trembled beneath me, unraveling with every touch.

His pleasure was the only thing that mattered right now. Watching him lose all control because of me—that was the only finish line I cared about crossing.

He wrapped his legs around my hips, pulling me deeper, claiming me in return. The energy between us shifted. This wasn't just me giving. He was taking too.

It was incredible.

It didn't take long, though, before I couldn't hold back the inevitable.

"You ready?" I asked as I closed my grip on him and stroked in time with my thrusts.

That did it. His body locked up, the cords in his neck standing out, and a hoarse cry ripped from his throat. He spilled his load over my fist and onto his stomach. His muscles clamped down on me, rhythmic and relentless. Pleasure unfurled, white-hot and consuming, dragging a groan from deep in my chest as I came.

For long minutes, all I could hear was my own heartbeat and our panting. When I gathered enough strength to shift off him, he made a sound of protest.

I lay next to him, and he rolled to his side. Theo's fingers caressed me as he snuggled close, like he wasn't ready to let me go.

I wasn't ready to let go either.

In my previous relationships, physical intimacy had always carried a layer of analytical distance—a part of me quietly measuring, adjusting, making sure my partner was satisfied. With Theo, that part didn't disappear, but it no longer stood between us. I was still learning him, cataloging every sound and shiver, but I was in the moment too—swept up with him, not just holding the reins.

I was consumed.

By him.

By the sheer, overwhelming power of giving and receiving in equal measure.

"You're thinking too much," Theo whispered, his voice wrecked. His hand traced a shaky pattern on my damp chest.

I turned my head to look at him. His eyes were half-closed, his expression satiated and tender.

"Actually," I admitted, surprised by the truth of it, "I'm not thinking at all." A chuckle escaped me. "That's terrifyingly new."

He smiled against my shoulder. "The algorithm didn't predict that particular outcome, huh?"

"Not even close."

---

LATER, as we lay tangled in his sheets, lazily making out, Theo abruptly stopped. He propped himself on one elbow to look at me with unusual seriousness.

"I need to tell you something. About my book."

I tensed. "What about it?"

"I'm completely rewriting it. Instead of what I'd planned, it'll focus on how technology creates opportunities for connection without determining its authenticity. How genuine relationships develop not from computational prediction but from mutual choice and engagement."

I recognized the shift for what it was—and what it could mean. "Your publisher might not accept such a fundamental change."

"They might not. But I can't write something I no longer believe just to fulfill a contract."

"And what do you believe now?"

"That what's happened between us is real," he said simply. "That it began with algorithmic suggestion but transcended that origin through our choice and connection. That technology created an opportunity we might have missed, but what followed was authentically human."

His articulation matched the understanding I'd been reaching through my own analysis.

"I might lose the book contract." A hint of uncertainty entered his voice. "Which would be professionally inconvenient."

"I might lose board support before the IPO." I surprised myself with how little that prospect troubled me anymore. "Which would be financially significant."

Theo's hand found. "Are we crazy? Risking professional standing for... whatever this is?"

"Perhaps," I admitted. "But I've run the cost-benefit analysis extensively."

He laughed, the sound warming something in my chest. "Of course you have. And what was your conclusion?"

"That some variables can't be quantified but matter more than those that can." I interlaced our fingers. "Connection like this is rare enough to justify significant risk. And that I'd rather face professional challenges with you than professional success without you."

His expression softened into something I was still learning to recognize—vulnerability without fear, intimacy without calculation.

"That's probably the most romantic thing anyone has ever said to me." He leaned closer. "Especially coming from someone who processes emotions through statistical analysis."

"The non-analytical way to say this is, I love you, Theo Barrett."

His smile lit something in me that no algorithm could have predicted but that felt more certain than any computational match.

"And I love you, Zach Mendez."

# 21

Theo

THE KNOT in my stomach tightened with each adjustment I made to my tie.

I checked my reflection in the green room mirror and barely recognized myself. Vivian and Zach had both weighed in on my wardrobe—separately, they claimed, though their verdict was the same. It was one thing to show up to cover an event in my usual T-shirt and sport coat, but the guy about to walk onstage and deliver this talk apparently needed to be dressed up.

I wasn't convinced. Shouldn't I be able to give a speech in clothes that didn't make me feel like I was cosplaying someone else's idea of respectable?

Five hundred people waited out there. Tech

journalists. Academics. Critics who once nodded along with my takedowns of algorithmic dating.

Now? Now I was...

"You look fine," Vivian said, pulling me out of my thoughts. She looked up from her phone. "Stop fidgeting. Undermines the confident intellectual image."

"I'm not looking to cultivate an image," I muttered.

This wasn't just another talk. My objectivity was up for debate before I'd even spoken a word. Could I stand up there and talk about nuance when my own life had become the primary case study?

Vivian studied me with a look of actual concern, which wasn't something I often saw from her. "The revised manuscript is excellent, by the way. You've convinced the publisher. The journey from critic to... whatever you are now... it's hooked them."

"Evolved skeptic?" The label didn't seem to fit. "Critical optimist?"

"Human being who changed his mind when faced with new evidence." She repeated the publicity angle the marketing department was considering. A reminder of the tightrope I was walking.

There was a sharp rap on the door, and a production assistant peered in. "Five minutes, Mr. Barrett."

Vivian gathered her things. "Break a leg. Metaphorically."

Alone, the silence hummed. I pulled out my phone, and the screen lit up. A perfectly timed message from Zach.

Zach: *Ready?*

My fingers trembled slightly typing back.

Theo: *As ready as anyone can be to acknowledge publicly they weren't entirely right.*

His response was instantaneous.

Zach: *Intellectual integrity is being willing to revise when evidence requires it. You taught me that. I know you're going to be great. See you after.*

Warmth spread through my chest, leveling out the anxiety.

He got it. He was having similar issues.

We'd spent the last month navigating the fallout. Our professional lives hadn't imploded, but we each had things to address in our own way. This Tech-Ethics conference felt like the right place for me to tell my story.

I made the quick walk to the side of the stage where I glimpsed the nearly full seating area. I found Zach. Had he chosen that spot so I could see him from here? Third row, aisle seat. With Trina and Riley next to him, Zach sat with the perfect stillness he deployed under pressure. He masked the tension

I knew vibrated just beneath the surface. This mattered to him. Maybe even more than to me.

I refocused myself by paying attention to the host's voice that boomed through the auditorium as he read my introduction.

"...and whose forthcoming book promises to deliver a unique perspective shaped by firsthand experience..."

This was it.

"Please welcome Theo Barrett."

I walked onto the stage, the lights hot and blinding. The applause was polite. I had notes in my jacket pocket, but I didn't take them out. Unscripted was the way to do this so that it came from the place within me where intellect wrestled with messy truth.

I leaned into the microphone, gripping the sides of the podium tight enough that my knuckles went white.

"Not long ago I would have stood before you with absolute certainty." My voice was steadier than I expected. "Certainty about the fundamental flaws in algorithmic approaches to human connection. Certainty about technology's inability to capture the illogical, glorious chaos of how people genuinely connect."

I found Zach in the crowd again, our eyes meeting for a moment, his gaze attentive and the corners of his mouth tipped in a small smile. A few rows behind him, I spotted Mom sitting with Vivian and Audry. With the two people I loved most in the audience, I had all the support I needed.

For the next twenty minutes, I laid it all out. Not a retraction, but an evolution of my thinking. Acknowledging the risks—bias baked into code, the illusion of certainty, the potential for misuse. But also acknowledging what I'd refused to see before. That thoughtfully designed systems, used transparently, could reveal possibilities. That algorithms didn't have to replace choice, but could, sometimes, inform it.

As I headed to the conclusion, my gaze returned to Zach. "These patterns that our own biases, our own limited social circles, might cause us to miss. They don't manufacture connection. They create opportunities. The spark, the decision to engage, to build something real despite the differences? That remains stubbornly, fiercely human."

I finished, and the silence stretched.

Then, applause broke out. It didn't come from everyone—I hadn't expected it to—but it was there, along with people who were nodding as if they understood.

Hands shot up. The host pointed to Jasmine

Vance, a sharp tech reporter from *The Verge*. Her expression was pure skepticism.

"Mr. Barrett, your evolved perspective seems convenient, given your public relationship with LoveLogic's founder." Her voice cut through the room. "How can you assure us of your journalistic integrity when you're romantically involved with the primary subject of your critique?"

I'd anticipated questions just like that one. Several recorders lifted higher to capture my response.

I didn't need to think long for the answer.

"That's a fair question." I focused on her. "What I can say is I'm committed to intellectual honesty. My book isn't an apology for algorithmic dating. It's an exploration of its complexities."

After another ten minutes of questions, the session ended. As I left the stage, adrenaline leaving a shaky residue, Zach was already waiting in the wings. His expression was something that looked suspiciously like pride. It wrapped around me as if he'd hugged me and said, "I love you."

"That was..." He searched for the precise word.

"Complicated?" I offered. A wry smile formed on my lips.

"I was going to say courageous." His hand found mine, a brief, grounding squeeze before dropping away as the first wave of reporters approached with more questions. "Not everyone can publicly revise their narrative."

We stood side-by-side, an unlikely pair fielding query after query. Zach, precise and calm, detailing LoveLogic's transparency measures. Me, articulating the tightrope walk between critique and personal experience.

"From adversaries to partners challenging the industry," one reporter remarked. There was a hint of amusement in his voice. "Very rom-com."

"Speaking of a challenge," another cut in. They held out their recorder to Zach. "LoveLogic's IPO? Pushed back after the anomaly disclosure, right?"

"We're proceeding on a revised timeline, incorporating enhanced user understanding features." He didn't mention the bruising board fights, Daniel Park's near-successful coup, or the precariousness of his own position. Only the validation of the positive market reaction to his transparency gamble had solidified his leadership.

Eventually, the crowd thinned, and Vivian and my mom approached.

"You were amazing," Mom said as she hugged me. "I'm so proud of you."

"Thank you. That means a lot." I returned her embrace.

Vivian held her tablet aloft as if in victory. "I just heard from the publisher." She angled the screen so I could read the email. "They've developed a possible title change based on what they heard today: *Algorithm for Love*. Pre-orders are spiking just from the buzz around your talk."

"It hasn't even been an hour yet." I scanned the enthusiastic message. It was a relief. It'd been hard enough to sell them on my concept. I'd worried about what might happen to the book if this didn't go well.

"They also want to set up joint interviews," Vivian continued.

I glanced at Zach. A slight nod was is only response.

"We'll consider it," I told Vivian. "But we'd want to focus on intellectual and ethical considerations, not tabloid-style personal details."

She nodded and was already typing. "The idea of a companion piece was also floated. From Zach so he can give his perspective."

A spark of interest lit Zach's eyes. "Interesting. We can talk about that too. We'll have to coordinate that, and the joint interview, with Trina of course."

"Of course," Vivian said. Her phone rang. "I've got to take this. I'll catch up with you two later."

"I think you've made her day," Mom said as Vivian walked away. "I'll leave you two to it. I'm sure you have lots of people to talk to still." She gave me and Zach hugs. "I'll see you both on Sunday."

As she left us, we didn't seek out more people, but instead headed to the balcony that was connected to the auditorium's lobby. We looked out as the afternoon light turned the skyscrapers golden. The air was cool, but warmth radiated from Zach as he stood next to me, our shoulders touching.

"So, you're considering authorship? I thought code was the only thing you wrote."

"I've been keeping notes. It started during our dates, and now I've got pages of personal reflections alongside algorithm refinements. Dr. Kostas even encouraged me to articulate the human considerations behind the tech."

I smiled at him, and the smile he gave me in return made my heart flutter. He continued to surprise me in the best ways.

Our phones shattered the moment. Mine buzzed first, followed within seconds by his.

"This has barely stopped since I turned on as I walked off the stage." I pulled the offending device from my pocket. "Would be irresponsible to leave it off for the rest of the night?"

Zach swiped on his screen. "That's better. Custom notifications activated."

"I should do that. My phone doesn't usually

blow up like this." I scanned some of the messages. "What are you seeing? I'm getting roughly half accolades, half accusations."

"Mine's similar. More investor inquiries, fewer integrity complaints." Zach turned to face me, and the light catching in his brown eyes drew me in. "I suppose we should go to the reception. More pointed questions likely await."

I shrugged. "We probably have to give them what they want. It'll be practice for those joint interviews Vivian mentioned."

He studied me, that unnervingly perceptive gaze he had when making an analysis. "You seem more... settled. More than I expected."

"I am." I took his hands in mine. "Standing up there, laying out the whole tangled journey... I don't have to keep two versions of myself anymore."

"Integration rather than opposition," he echoed. There was a hint of satisfaction in his voice. "Exactly what the complementary trait analysis identified."

"And I'm glad we explored that potential." I smiled and leaned in to kiss him.

I didn't know how Zach would react to being kissed in public, but he closed the distance, kissed me back, and wrapped me in a hug. It wasn't heated, just steady and certain. The kind of kiss that made me think about all the moments still to come.

# EPILOGUE

Zach

Six months later

Rows of perfectly aligned champagne flutes gleamed under the subtle lighting that had been installed in the lobby of LoveLogic's headquarters.

The IPO celebration preparations were proceeding with military precision, exactly as Trina and I had specified. I adjusted my new glasses—thinner frames that Theo insisted suited my face better—and checked the time.

Sixteen hours until the opening bell.

I moved through the space, mentally cataloging details while the setup crew worked around me. The journey here had been longer, more complex than planned, but the revised path led to a stronger destination. The initial valuation projections exceeded expectations by twenty-three percent. Investor confidence was at unprecedented levels. User trust metrics showed sustained growth. Transparency had proven strategically sound rather than just ethically necessary.

"Everything looks perfect." Trina stood beside me, checking items off of her tablet screen. "The only thing missing right now is the ice sculpture. It'll be here an hour before we open the doors in the morning." Her tone shifted to teasing. "You know, I still think an actual representation of the compatibility visualization is a bit much."

"The three-dimensional rendering helps stakeholders conceptualize the Barrett Protocol's integration of human choice and algorithmic guidance." A small smile escaped me. "Theo also thought it would be 'amusingly on-brand.'"

Trina laughed. "You realize half our development team still can't believe we named our flagship feature after the critic who once called us 'emotional strip-miners.'"

"Former critic, now current consultant in algorithmic ethics," I corrected. "The Barrett Protocol represents what his critique helped us develop—a system that enhances human choice rather than attempting to replace it."

The name started as an internal joke, but it stuck. It defined LoveLogic's augmented choice approach—algorithmic insights paired with emphasized user agency. Trina and the marketing department resisted, but consumer testing showed the name enhanced credibility, signaling our evolution through critique.

Trina's phone buzzed. She glanced at the screen and smiled. "The final trading range is approved. We're a go for tomorrow. Congratulations, Zach."

"Congratulations to us all. Getting here was very much a team effort."

Relief washed through me, followed by the awareness of the climb still ahead. The IPO was a hard-won peak, but there was a lot of work to do to keep up the momentum.

Six months ago, this moment seemed increasingly unlikely—the anomaly disclosure, the contentious board meetings, Daniel Park leading the faction demanding my replacement, citing "compromised objectivity" and "transparency obsession."

Trina continued, scrolling her checklist. "And Daniel's resignation announcement is scheduled to go out thirty minutes after the opening bell."

"Good timing." I kept my satisfaction in check, knowing Daniel's influence on the industry and investors wouldn't vanish overnight. Trina and I had talked a lot about striking the right public tone regarding his departure and how it solidified our new direction.

Multiple clashes over the Barrett Protocol implementation finally cost Daniel the board's confidence. His replacement—a former psychology professor with tech industry experience—represented the balance that now defined LoveLogic.

"I think we're done here." I surveyed the space once more.

Trina looked at me, smiling. "You should go home, Zach. Get some rest before the biggest day of your professional life."

I nodded.

Theo would be waiting at my apartment—our apartment, increasingly, though not yet officially. The boundary blurred daily. His books colonized my shelves. His vintage record player sat beside my precision sound system, its occasional warm static a counterpoint to digital silence. His casual approach to time softened my rigid scheduling.

"One more thing we'll announce tomorrow," Trina said as I gathered my things. "The board approved the Mendez Foundation funding. The full endowment was ok'd for the algorithmic ethics research center, including Theo's input on the governance structure."

This mattered even more than the IPO.

The foundation was a commitment to evolving technology with human values centered. It would fund the study of ethical algorithm implementation —transparency, autonomy, equity.

"Thank you, Trina. For everything. Not just prep to get us public, but your support throughout... all of this." I gestured vaguely, encompassing the transformation of the past several months. "I know I haven't always made it easy."

"Getting sentimental, Zach?"

"I do have a heart. Though rumors would suggest otherwise."

Her warm laughter followed me to the elevator. The doors closed, reflecting my image in the polished metal—same tailored suit, same grooming, but someone who had become more present, connected, and happy.

THE DOOR OPENED before my key touched the lock. Theo stood there, expression bright with barely contained excitement. I immediately noticed his t-shirt. No band logo emblazoned across his chest this time—just the Barrett Protocol, identical to the one the artist had carved into ice.

I didn't have words.

"Like it?" Theo finally asked.

"How? What? It's..."

Theo led me inside.

"That's amazing. I would've never thought to put it on a shirt. It looks incredible."

"Trina hooked me up with the rendering. There's one in the bedroom for you, too."

I ran my hand over the blue and gold image, while also relishing the feel of his chest under the fabric. "Thanks. I love it." I planted a soft kiss on his lips, which were still stretched in a smile.

"Can I show you something else?"

"Of course."

"They're here." He pulled me into the dining room.

On the table sat a box. From its open top, a book peeked out.

"Advance copies." Theo was practically vibrating. "Delivered an hour ago."

He reached in, withdrew one and placed it in my hands. It had a striking cover, with binary code transitioning into handwritten text. *Algorithm for Love: From Skeptic to Partner in the Digital Age.* Theo's name was prominent under the title, and below that was an ethicist's endorsement quote.

"Open it," he urged.

I flipped through the pages until I got to the dedication.

*For Zach, who proved that the most meaningful connections develop not from algorithmic certainty but from human choice—and that sometimes, the algorithm just creates the opportunity for those choices to begin.*

My throat tightened. "It's perfect." I met his gaze.

"You didn't read the acknowledgments yet." He gestured at the book and looked as excited as a kid at Christmas.

I turned to the back and scanned through the usual thanks to people who'd worked with him, like Vivian and Audry. Then, I found my name again.

*My deepest gratitude goes to Zach Mendez, whose willingness to engage with critique rather than dismiss it reflects the truest form of intellectual integrity. His evolution from algorithmic certainty to embracing human complexity paralleled my journey from skepticism to nuanced understanding. Our story proves that genuine connection develops not from computational prediction but through choice, vulnerability, and the willingness to see beyond initial positions to the complementary strengths beneath. He remains both my greatest challenge and my most meaningful choice.*

I looked at him again. Theo's words, forever on the page, landed like a counterweight to my years of guardedness. Fragility and certainty warred in his expression.

"I know we don't often use words like this. But I wanted it in print. Permanent. Unchangeable."

"Using the oldest information technology to document the newest." My voice caught just enough to betray how much what he wrote had hit me. "Very on-brand for you."

"Thought you'd appreciate the symmetry." His smile accelerated my pulse.

"I do. Thank you. All this—your words, the t-shirt."

I set the book down carefully and moved toward him, pulled by the gravity that had only intensified since we'd become a couple. What I had to do next scared me—I couldn't afford to get it wrong. The gift in my pocket wasn't complicated, but the meaning behind it was everything.

"I have something for you too," I said. "Though not quite as published or permanent."

"More permanent might be concerning," he teased. "You haven't secretly tattooed my compatibility metrics on your arm, have you?"

"Um, no. Nothing that extreme." I couldn't help but shake my head and grin at him. As I reached into my pocket for the small box I'd carried for three days, my fingers were clumsy for a moment. A brief flicker of my distancing tactics tried to surface. Luckily, those were easier to push away than they used to be. "Though this might be more significant in some ways."

His expression shifted as he saw the slim container.

I opened it to reveal a simple keycard. "This is a key to our new place. I've purchased the penthouse in the Westview building. It's empty—no furniture, no design elements, nothing predetermined."

Theo took it, examining the small rectangle in uncharacteristic silence.

"I know how important your space is." I clung to the words I'd rehearsed, using them to steady my nerves. "Your books, your records, your organized chaos. This apartment—" I gestured around the room. "—has always been mine, designed to my specifications. Even with your additions, it remains fundamentally my space that you occupy."

"And the new place would be...?" His voice held careful neutrality.

"Ours," I said simply. "A blank slate we design together. Not my precision with your spontaneity tacked on, or your chaos trimmed to fit my order. Something built as one from the very start."

Understanding dawned in his expression.

"You're asking me to officially move in with you. By suggesting we create an entirely new space."

I met his gaze. "Yes. I know it's a significant step. I've analyzed the potential complications and benefits." My breath hitched. "Though the core variable remained stubbornly outside anything that could be in a spreadsheet."

He laughed, tension breaking. "Of course you have. Spreadsheets? Decision matrices?"

"Several." I smiled despite myself. "I ultimately decided based on non-quantifiable variables."

"Which were?" He stepped closer.

"That I want to build something with you." The directness was no longer foreign. It came naturally, as if it had always been dormant within me.

Theo leaned in, his hand warm against my face. "Has anyone ever told you that you're surprisingly romantic for a man who processes emotions through statistical modeling?"

"Only you. Repeatedly. And with increasing frequency over the past six months."

His kiss was steady, sure, and full of the trust we'd rebuilt. It wasn't just something I offered him— it was the foundation we'd built side by side. And its strength unshakable.

We held each other tight, and when we broke

apart, Theo leaned his forehead against mine. My pulse raced waiting for his answer.

"Yes," he said. "To the new place. To building something as a couple. To whatever completely unpredictable life we create."

Relief and joy settled as my hands slowly ran over the familiar contours of his back. What once felt like navigating unexplored territory now carried the comfort of coming home while still knowing there were always new experiences to explore together.

Tomorrow would bring professional validation. Tonight gave me something rarer: the certainty that the most meaningful algorithm wasn't coded into LoveLogic, but into the life we chose every day. A pattern balancing structure and spontaneity, precision and intuition, analysis and emotion—a choice no computer could capture.

"I love you," Theo said.

"Love you, too." I kissed him, and he deepened it, our connection sparking like it always did. I held him close, choosing him now and forever.

## THE END

In the story, Zach and Theo never make it to their final dinner date. Want to know what happens when they finally complete *Their Four Date Experiment?*

Well, we wrote a special bonus epilogue where you can get all the romantic details!

You can download it for free at: WilliamGayheart.com/FourDateExtra.

Thanks for coming along for the ride with Zach and Theo — from intellectual sparring partners to something much closer. Their story about finding connection across philosophical divides felt especially timely in our tech-saturated world, where we're always juggling digital convenience and real, human moments.

Writing these two stubborn, brilliant men was a blast. The professional rivals and opposites attract tropes gave us the perfect way to explore how old wounds can shape our strongest beliefs. We loved watching them poke at each other's certainties and slowly realize how their strengths complemented one another.

Hope you enjoyed it.

— Jeff & Will

# ALSO BY WILLIAM GAYHEART

- *A Match Made in Santorini*
- *Behind the Bar*
- *Bought by His Brother's Best Friend*
- *Branding His Wyoming Heart*
- *His Trainer's Touch*
- *Protecting His Playboy Prince*
- *Sweet Spring Fling*

## *Bigger Is Best* series

- *His Big Hometown Cowboy*
- *His Big Holiday Firefighter*

# ABOUT WILLIAM GAYHEART

William Gayheart is a proud queer author.

He is an expert overthinker and nap enthusiast, who writes the kinds of stories he loves to read—sweet gay romances with a little bit of heat, and a whole lot of heart.

## *Hockey Hearts* **Romance Series**

- *The Hockey Player's Heart* (co-written with Will Knauss)
- *The Hockey Player's Snow Day*
- *Keeping Kyle* (A Hockey Allies Bachelor Bid Romance)
- *Head in the Game*
- *Rivals*
- *Taking a Shot at Love*
- *Skating Back to You* (A Hockey Hearts and On Stage crossover)
- *Checked by His Teammate*
- *Pride by the Book* (A Love in Maplewood Romance)

## *On Stage* **Romance Series**

- *Dancing for Him*
- *Love's Opening Night*

## **More Romance**

- *Bicycle Built for Two*
- *Room Service*

- *Somewhere on Mackinac*
- *Summer Heat*

---

## Young Adult Titles

### *Codename: Winger* series

Available in ebook, paperback, and audiobook (narrated by Kirt Graves).

- *Tracker Hacker* (includes the bonus short story *A Very Winger Christmas*)
- *Schooled*
- *Audio Assault*
- *Netminder*

---

## Non-Fiction

- *Content for Everyone: A Practical Guide for Creative Entrepreneurs to Produce Accessible and Usable Web Content* (co-written with Michele Lucchini)

# ABOUT JEFF ADAMS

Jeff Adams has written stories since he was in middle school and became a published author in 2009 when his first short stories were released. He writes gay romance and LGBTQ young adult fiction...and there's usually a hockey player at the center of the story.

Jeff lives in central California with his husband of more than twenty-five years, Will. Some of Jeff's favorite things include the musicals *Rent* and [*title of show*], and the Detroit Red Wings and Pittsburgh Penguins hockey teams. Of course, he also loves to read.

In his day job, Jeff is a digital accessibility expert and he consults with companies about making their digital experiences accessible. He's brought that knowledge to creative entrepreneurs with *Content for Everyone*, a book which helps creatives understand what they can do to create content that is accessible and usable by everyone.

Learn more about Jeff, his books at JeffAdams Writes.com.

www.ingramcontent.com/pod-product-compliance
Lightning Source LLC
Chambersburg PA
CBHW071200100726
47908CB00002B/450